Broken Spirit

DEFIANCE

SKYE MACKINNON

Peryton Press

BROKEN SPIRIT

USA TODAY BESTSELLING AUTHOR

SKYE MACKINNON

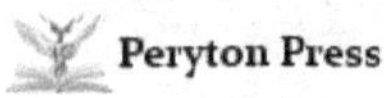

Peryton Press

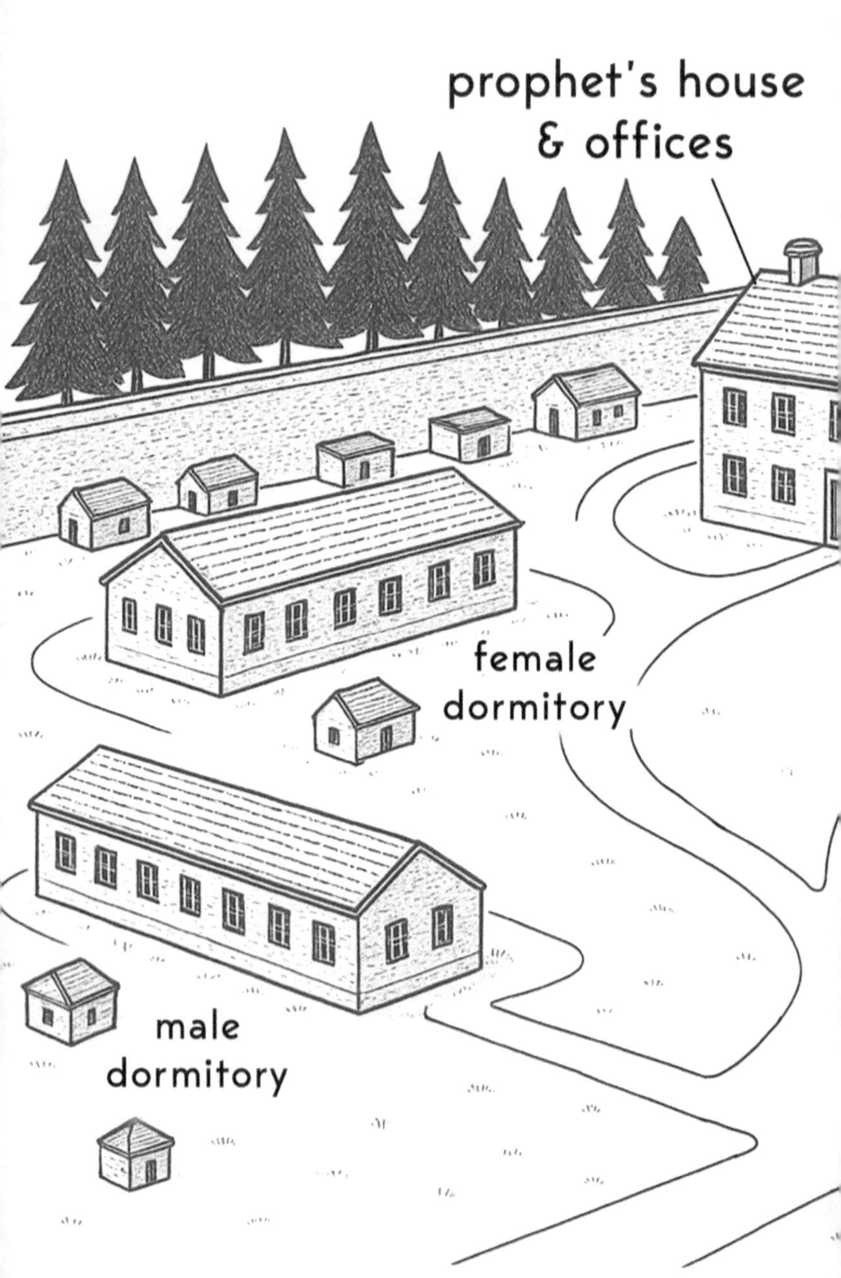

prophet's house
& offices
female
dormitory
male
dormitory

the compound

Contents

Author's Note

****Trigger warning: This is a dark story that contains violence, sexual abuse, mentions of suicide and death. Read at your own discretion.****

This story is also available as audiobook and paperback!

Subscribe to Skye's newsletter and get a free book as a thank you:
skyemackinnon.com/newsletter

For the Flock. I'd never have been able to write this book without your emotional support.

Prologue

he sound of the whip being unfurled is worse than the pain to come. The tingling of anticipation is running over my skin, preparing my nerve endings for the beating that he's about to unleash on my naked body.

Pain is salvation.

I steel my mind like he taught me.

Discipline leads to redemption.

He only wants to help. That's why he's going to whip me.

Suffering brings peace.

Without pain, I won't be able to be freed of this mortal

world. I won't be able to ascend with the Prophet and the others. The pain is necessary.

I take a deep breath, readying myself.

"Begin."

Part One

One

His ugly scent still hangs in the air even after he's long gone. It's all over my skin, reminding me of what just happened. I want to cry and have a shower, but the first won't do any good and the second is forbidden. It's still two more days until I'm allowed my next shower.

I pull my blanket closer, but then throw it away when its touch reminds me of the marks he's left on me. It's too rough, just like his hands. I breathe in deep through my mouth, but can't stop a bit of his scent getting trapped in my nose. His breath always reminds me of something rotten, something so dead inside that it's almost impossible to hide. But he hides it well. To the others, he's a holy man, a Prophet. To me, he's the devil.

At least he'll be busy until later today. Time for me to prepare for his next beating. It's one of those days when he's angry and needs someone to let out his frustrations on. He told me once that with every mark on my skin, his anger gets less. It's a sign for him that he's working on it.

That's what he sees it as. Dealing with his problems. I'm the canvas to paint his anger onto.

A few more hours until he's back. It's harder knowing what's to come than when it's one of his impulsive attacks. Those I can usually avoid by staying in the company of the other women. He doesn't do it in front of people. He's their leader, he needs to show how he's the perfect person. The chosen one. The Prophet. The King.

Inside though, he's rotten to the core. Nothing royal in there. Just hate and violence and anger and pride. All the sins he preaches against are somewhere in him. Maybe that's why he's so passionate about eradicating them. If everybody else is without sin, maybe he will be, too.

I wish he'd allow us some cream to put on the bruises, but that's forbidden. When I first moved here, I thought it was a good thing that cosmetics are banned in the compound. Now, I see it differently. If he puts bruises on me, he should give me something to treat them.

He always makes sure that the bruises stay below the neckline. I'm not allowed to wear revealing shirts anyway, none of us are. Our simple uniform includes a long-sleeved blouse and a skirt that reaches our ankles. Together with our shorn heads, we're hard to tell apart. That's how it's supposed to be. We're all one family, one community, where nobody is better than the others. Except for Andros, of course.

Twenty women, all thin as sticks, heads bowed, quiet and demure. But still, I'm different, even though I don't want to be. I'm wearing a golden circlet on my shaved head, telling everyone that I'm the Prophet's wife. His Princess. He's the King, but he is so far above us all that it would be silly to call me his queen. No, I'm the Princess, and that keeps me apart from the other women in the compound.

Only at dawn and dusk, when we recite the words of our community, we're all the same. When the fog hangs deep in the valley, we assemble in the clearing in the centre of the village and chant together:

Discipline leads to redemption.
Suffering brings peace.
Obedience inspires happiness.
Pain is salvation.
The Angel is our shield and our refuge.

It's the mantra I hear every day. I say it every day. And once, I believed it. Maybe I still do.

Back then, I said those words with fervour and passion. But that all changed long ago and now, it's empty words for me. I say them because it's expected of me. Because I will be punished if I don't. As the Princess, I need to be an example, both in good deeds and in my punishments. My husband likes to show everyone how women should be treated. The bruises stay beneath my clothes, but there are other ways to punish and humiliate. Andros knows every single one of them.

I once admired him for his intelligence and creativity. Now I fear him for coming up with yet another method of punishment. But then I remember that I deserve it, and it hurts less.

We all deserve to suffer.

Suffering brings peace.

Does something become true if you say it often enough? Does the universe listen and make it so?

If so, then I will be at peace. I have suffered a lot. Not just me, we all have. Suffering is at the core of our community. We built it up from scratch, we fought with the inhospitable land to survive. There are no modern conveniences out here; we are on our own. Suffering has been with us from day one.

How long has it been since then? Five years? Six? Time has lost its meaning.

Some days, I'm still happy I live here, away from society, together with men and women sworn to a simpler life. Other days, all I want to do is run.

Pain flares up around my right ankle and I bite back a groan. It always does that when I think of leaving. The thin silver bracelet he once put on me has merged with my flesh, burned into my skin. It was the first and only time I ever tried to run away.

He said that if I ever tried it again, he'd use the same blowtorch on my head until the golden circlet I'm forced to wear melts and permanently becomes part of me.

I put a hand on my ankle, the coolness of my skin a soothing relief for the pain that isn't really there. It's just a memory. The pain everywhere else is very real, though. Why am I focussing on my ankle when my stomach feels like a car has run me over?

It's probably some kind of self-preservation mechanism.

I roll to my other side to take the pressure off my bruised ribs. Spots dance along my vision as the pounding in my head starts anew.

How did a life without pain feel like? Was I happier back then?

We're taught to forget the past, to focus on the present and on our future. Especially on our future. Everything we do is to make sure that we'll transcend once we leave this life behind. Andros says that so far, he is the only one who's ready to ascend, but he's staying behind to make sure that we reach the same level of preparation. He's generous like that, sharing his wisdom and knowledge. Other Prophets may have just left, preferring to be with the Angel.

Not Andros, though. He cares for all of us, his flock, even though his methods can be rough. At least I think that's what he believes.

I'm not quite sure if I believe it. I've not known what's real and what isn't for a long time. I hope that Paradise is real. That way, all what we're going through is going to be worth it.

Discipline leads to redemption.

Our daily struggles, the punishments, the harsh rules, it's all to prepare us for ascension. Right now, we're not worthy of the Angel's attention. But soon, we will be. Andros will make sure of it.

I focus on that thought. No matter how much I despise Andros, he is the Prophet. The pain will only be temporary.

But it's so hard to believe. Everything hurts, even lying on the hard wooden floor is painful. I think he may have cracked my ribs again. Every breath is an ache in my chest, but I'm not ready to stop breathing yet. I'm not ready.

A gentle knock on the door has me sit up.

Petal enters, searching the room for me before her eyes spot me in the corner.

"How bad is it?" she asks quietly and hurries to me.

"It's been worse," I reply with a grimace and take the glass of water she's offering me.

"Pain is salvation," Petal says, her expression full of hope and conviction. She may be kind to me, but she's also one of Andros's most passionate followers. She was one of the first, and likely she'll be the first of his flock to ascend, too.

She takes back the glass and hands me a wet cloth. We're not allowed to put salve on our wounds, but at least the coolness of the water will provide some relief. I start patting my forehead to remove the sweat and the tears. If Andros sees me like this, weak and frail, it will only make him angry.

While I begin to gently rub away the blood on my shoulders, Petal takes another cloth and cleans my back. Every single touch hurts, but it's a better pain than that of the whip, because it's not intentional.

"He'll be late," the older woman informs me. "There are three new applicants and he's decided to interview them right away. Three men, I think, but I only got a quick look before he told me to look after you."

He didn't send her because he's kind. No, he wants a clean canvas for later to continue his painting. The existing stripes of wounds and barely healed scars don't bother him, but dried blood does. It looks dirty, he says, so he always sends one of the other women to make me clean again.

"Where are they from?" I ask her, but she clucks her tongue in disapproval. Their past doesn't matter. We shouldn't question where they come from, just where they're going.

"If he agrees to take them in as novices, we'll have an assembly tonight," she informs me instead of answering my question.

I suppress a sigh. If there's an assembly, I have to leave our hut, which means wearing my scratchy, heavy robe on my open wounds. It's going to be even more painful than it is now.

The last time we had new people join our community is months ago. Maybe even a year. Now that we're completely self-sufficient, we don't communicate with the outside world any longer. Andros is the only one who leaves occasionally to buy supplies. Nobody knows we exist. Sometimes, Andros talks about wanting to spread the message of the Angel so that more people can be saved, but then he decides that we're enough followers. If we'd accept new people, it would take them long to adjust and to learn. Our own ascension would be delayed, and Andros wouldn't like that. He's stayed here with us for too long already. He wants to ascend and join the Angel, just like we all do.

"Let's pray," Petal says, and sits down by my side, her hands on her knees, turned upward so that the blessings of the Angel can flow into her. I take the same position, trying not to wince as pain flows through me. This beating was worse than the ones before, and I know it's going to take a while to heal.

"Angel, your words are salvation," Petal begins and I join her, my mind focussing on the mantras and forgetting the pain.

The bell is loud and doesn't stop ringing for several minutes. I try to ignore it, but the sound hammers against my sore head until I can't stand it any longer. I get up from my thin mattress on the floor and put on my white robe. It's assembly, and we don't wear our normal clothes for that.

Petal left after our prayers and I got to sleep for a bit, but it seems that my time of rest is over. At least Andros hasn't had time to pay me another visit.

I carefully lift the robe over my head and let it fall on me, hoping that it won't reopen my wounds. They seem to have closed while I slept, but the blood on my sheets tells the story of my agony.

I stay barefoot; we're only allowed to wear shoes in the winter.

Warm evening light welcomes me as I step out of my hut. The sun is low behind the hills in the distance, its last light bathing the compound in orange hues. The sunsets always are spectacular here. In a moment, the sun will disappear behind the hills with one final goodbye, a bright crest on the top of the mountains, before only its light remains.

The bell finally stops, and I hurry towards the community hall in the centre of our fenced village. The fence is to keep others out, or so Andros says. We're living in the middle of nowhere, so there are wild animals that we need to prevent from invading our home.

Almost everyone is assembled in the hall already, and I

take a seat at the back, kneeling on the thin mat covering the ground. We only use the hall for assemblies and in the winter; now during the summer we do our prayers outside, despite the midges.

Andros is standing at the front, easy to see as everyone else is kneeling. Next to him are three men, already wearing the red robes of novices. That was quick. Usually new people take several days to bring their belongings here and to say goodbye to the world. Once you're here, you don't get to stay in touch with your relatives. It's a final decision, and most aren't brave enough to make it.

We are the steadfast ones, the loyal followers who've made that decision. We've forsaken all worldly pleasures and connections and our only purpose in life is to serve the Angel and prepare to join him.

I keep my head bowed but sneak a look at the men nonetheless. Their faces are hard to see under their hoods, but one of them has long black hair falling to his chest. He's going to have to cut it off soon. I almost pity him for it; it must have taken him years to grow his hair that long. He has a shaggy beard as well, barely visible under his hood. The other two are clean-shaven, but that's all I can make out. One of them is a little broader, but it's muscles, not fat, as far as I can see from here. The other two are quite thin, or at least athletic. That's good, they won't mind the lack of big meals then. In the summer, we only eat twice a day, once before sunrise and once after sunset. I've got used to the clenching feeling of hunger in my stomach, but that's only after years of living like this.

The large doors close behind me and Andros steps forward, looking down at his followers.

"Welcome, flock of the Angel," he says in his loud, booming voice that easily reaches every corner of the hall. "We're assembled tonight to greet our newest members and welcome them into our midst. I will decide their names later, so for now, they remain nameless. The cleansing ceremony will be tomorrow. Bryan, Eamon, Jeremy, you'll be assisting them in the process."

Three men get up from the floor and bow deeply, before kneeling back down.

I remember my own cleansing process and repress a shudder. It's not a pleasant experience, but it's necessary to get rid of our mortal sins and prepare our minds and bodies for the Angel.

Andros smiles widely as he looks at the new men. "You have made the right decision to come here, friends. We will welcome you with open hearts and open arms, and will lead you onto the right path. Once you have your new names, you will be given a hut to share until you build your own ones. You will wear the red robes of novices and study the sacred texts. When you're ready, I will test you, and if you're found worthy, you will be given the white robes of the chosen ones."

The men don't say anything, but they all nod to show that they've understood. That will please Andros. He doesn't like it when people ask questions.

"Sit," he tells them, pointing at an empty row at the front. It's reserved for novices and nobody has been sitting there for a long time. "I don't expect you to take part in our worship tonight, as you don't know the words and rituals yet, but I do expect you to study hard so you can become part of our community quickly."

Again, they remain quiet. They seem like the perfect recruits: silent, eager to learn, pliable. Andros will like them.

Two

My husband was too tired last night to continue his painting, so I got to sleep without new streaks of blood staining my bedsheets. When I wake up, his arm is wrapped around my waist, pressing me to him possessively. His chest is hard against the broken skin on my back. When he wakes, there will be blood on his chest. He will punish me for it.

I close my eyes and try to get back to sleep, get some rest before the new pain arrives, but it's a fruitless endeavour. I'm awake, and the anticipation of his next beating is rising up in me, choking my heart.

Suffering brings peace, I recite in my head, focussing on the words the Angel teaches us. Once we've ascended, we won't even remember all the pain we had to endure on the way to his kingdom. We will never feel pain again.

I concentrate on that thought, imagining the Paradise waiting for us. The endless pastures of golden grass, the two suns in the sky, the sounds of angelic choruses caressing my ears. That's how it's written and that's how it will be. This pain is just a test, nothing more. I have to get through it. I have to be stronger.

Andros grunts in his sleep and his grip on me loosens slightly. Is it worth trying to get up without him noticing? No, that might just increase the punishment. I stay where I am, feeling the movements of his chest on my sore back, breathing as shallowly as I can so he doesn't wake from the sound of my breath.

I open my eyes again and look around. The floor is rough, the wood taken straight from the forest without having been polished. When I first moved here, I loved the natural feel of it all, but once I got the first splinters in my bare feet, I rethought that sentiment. Dust is dancing in the sunlight streaming through the windows, and I make a mental note to clean the house later on. If Andros leaves me alone and without further injuries, I'll be able to sweep the hut, maybe even wipe the windows. Their plexiglass always looks dirty and streaked, no matter how much I try and clean them. Still, I won't give up trying. I'd love to have windows I can look through and not see impurities.

Andros grunts again and I stiffen.

Is he awake?

"Little dove," he whispers and his hand on my stomach moves, slowly running over my skin. I shiver in frightened anticipation of what's to come. This doesn't happen often, not anymore, but when it does... I close my eyes again and withdraw deep into myself, willing it to be over quickly.

He breathes in deep as his fingers reach between my legs.

"My frightened little bird..."

He chuckles and drives two fingers into me, surprising

me. I'm not wet at all and it hurts. I never get wet for him anymore. I gasp and he takes that as an invitation to wrap his other hand around my head and stuff his fingers into my mouth. His erection presses against my back, hard and ready to invade me.

I picture the Angel in my mind as he flips me onto my back and begins to take me like I'm his property.

Which I am. We all are.

We missed breakfast, but while Andros gets himself something from the communal kitchen, I have no such privileges. I've not felt this bad in ages. Hungry, in pain, dirty. I want a shower, but it's not shower day today. Tomorrow, I think. Until then, I will have to make do with washcloths and cold water. It amazes me that Andros wants me to be clean for him, but only allows us a shower every four days. I'm sure there's a reason for it, though.

I hurry to the office building. It's one of the more elaborate huts; it was built as a community effort and not by just one or two people, like most of the other houses. It also contains the library and a room for Andros to meet visitors. We don't get a lot of them, but sometimes there have been random family members coming to check on their relatives. Often, they think we're some kind of cult and want to 'rescue' their siblings or children, but Andros is good at explaining that we're not a cult. We're a community living in simple ways, working together towards a better tomorrow.

Andros is great with words. He knows exactly how to convey his messages in the best possible way. It's no wonder he charmed his way into my heart when we first met.

"You're late," Heather tells me as I step into the office.

"I'm sorry," I say quietly and take my seat next to her. My bum hurts when I sit, the bruises making themselves known. There's an ache between my legs, too, but I try to ignore that one. I should be grateful that Andros paid me attention this morning; many women in the community would be happy to be his partner. I know he visits some of them, and they see it as an honour to lie with the Prophet. For me it's different though. We're married and we used to have a romantic, loving relationship full of sweet gestures and gentle touches. That's gone now and the man sharing my bed and owning my body is a new one. Not my husband, but the Prophet.

Heather hands me a leather-bound book and a stack of paper. "We need to be quick, we only have one copy left and there are three new arrivals."

I nod and get to work, copying the Angel's message in my neat handwriting. We don't have electricity here, and therefore no computers and printers. We copy our books by hand, like the monks of old used to do. Heather and I were chosen because we have the prettiest handwriting.

I know the book by heart, but I still make sure to check every sentence before I write it down. If I make a mistake, I will have to start that page again. The three new men will want to start learning soon, and they won't be able to do that without their own copy of the Angel's words.

The sun warms my back as it ascends higher behind the hills and flows through the window behind me. It's a gentle embrace that I savour and commit to memory. I store all the beautiful moments and sensations in a large chest in my mind, to draw from in difficult times. Maybe I'll be able to keep these memories once I've ascended.

I only make a mistake once, and by the time the midday bell rings, I am about a third into the book I'm copying. Heather is slower than me, and she scowls when she sees how I have more completed pages lying on my table.

"I'll check for errors later," she announces and leaves the office hastily. I'm not sure why she wants to be at the prayers before everybody else, but she's always been a bit strange.

I righten my golden circlet and run a hand over my shaved head. Tomorrow, after my shower, I'll have to shave it again to make sure I stay clean for the Angel. He wants us all to be pure, not focussed on outer beauty but on the beauty within our hearts. The men are allowed to have short hair because they're not expected to be vain, and Andros can have his hair however he wants to. He's already proven to the Angel that he's ready to ascend and only stays behind for us.

When I leave the hut, I'm struck by the amount of activity going on outside. People are hurrying back and forth, bearing bowls and crates, and it takes me a moment to remember that they're preparing for the new arrivals' cleansing ceremony. The three men Andros chose last night will be helping the Prophet administer the cleansing, but everybody is expected to help with the preparations.

I head to the main square where the figure of the Angel is looking down on us from the pedestal he's standing on. Lacey, one of the first followers of the Prophet, was an artist in her previous life and made the statue for us, following Andros's precise description of the visions he'd seen the Angel in.

It's a beautiful statue and it always reminds me why we're living the way we do. To get close to him. To be with the Angel. To be worthy of his attention.

His golden hair is shimmering in the sunlight, giving him an even more divine appearance.

The bell rings again and slowly, people are forming a circle around the statue. Some are whispering the mantra, others have their eyes closed in meditation. Some days, Andros is too busy to lead us in prayer, but we all know the scriptures and rituals anyway, so we conduct the midday prayer ourselves.

Today though, he is here, together with the three new men in their bright red robes. They're looking at the Angel in wonder; it's probably the first time they've seen him.

When everyone is assembled, Andros sweeps his arms wide as if he's about to embrace us all.

"My children, welcome into our midst your new brothers: Martin, Noran and Owen."

He points at the three men one after the other. I suppress a smile. He's continuing his strange tradition of naming new arrivals in alphabetic order. He says the Angel tells him what to call new members of the community, but sometimes I suspect he just looks them up in a dictionary. I wonder what the name Noran means or why he's chosen that one. It's unusual. With women it's easy; most of us are named after flowers. Petal, Heather, Rose, Jasmine...

Not me, though. He called me Laya because it means music, and he met me when I was singing karaoke in a club.

I've never been a particularly good singer, but he told me my voice was divine and reminded me of the music he heard in his visions of the Angel.

Yet another reason why I'm different from the other women in the community.

"I would like to introduce you to some of my brothers and sisters," he tells the new men loudly. He points at me and beckons me to the centre of the circle. I hurry to follow his command and take my position by his side.

"My wife, Laya, the Princess of our family."

"Nice to meet you," one of the men says. Owen, perhaps? I'm not quite sure who's who. Andros frowns but smooths his expression immediately. The men will learn soon enough that no man is to address me. I'm Andros's and his alone.

"I have tasked her to copy the sacred texts for you. When will they be ready, dear?" Andros looks at me sternly and I swallow hard.

"Tomorrow, my Prophet," I reply, my eyes fixed on the ground.

"Make that tonight," he orders. I don't even try to protest. His word is what will be, even if I have to sit there and write faster than I've ever written before.

"Yes, my Prophet," I say demurely, but he's already ignoring me again.

He points at several people of the community and they all come forward and get introduced to the newbies.

I zone out, already picturing the pages I will have to copy. They won't be as beautiful as I would like them to be, but I will need to do what Andros commands.

The Prophet ends our session by reciting the sacred

mantra. I say the words loud and clear, fervently hoping that they're true.

Discipline leads to redemption.
Suffering brings peace.
Obedience inspires happiness.
Pain is salvation.
The Angel is our shield and our refuge.

The afternoon passes quickly and by the time the sun is beginning to set, I finally finish copying the final page of the book. My right hand is cramping, but the satisfaction I feel at managing to fulfil Andros's expectations is more important. He will be proud of me.

I put the pen to one side and get up, stretching. The healing wounds on my back are protesting the sudden movements, but after sitting in the same chair for hours, my muscles need the exercise.

Heather still has several pages to do. I wonder if I should offer to help her, but Andros wouldn't like it if there were two different styles in one book. He likes things orderly and accurately.

"See you later," I mutter, not wanting to disturb her.

I'm almost out of the door when she says, "Ooops," and the sound of a glass tumbling onto wood makes me swirl around.

Water is running over the table as if in slow motion, sinking deep into the paper I wrote on, letting the ink flow freely. I run back, ripping the ruined pages away from the water, but it's too late. Blue ink is dripping down on the table and on my robe, leaving stains that look a lot like the tears threatening to spill from my eyes.

"Such a pity," Heather says cheerily. "You'll have to start again."

Angel, give me strength. I let the paper fall back onto the table. My luck has it that a few blue ink drops fall onto Heather's page and she snarls.

"I'm going to tell Andros," she announces and gets up, taking the pages she's finished with her. As if I was going to destroy them like she did mine. No, I'd never do that.

I don't know why Heather hates me this much. Or is she this evil to everyone? Maybe it's because we're all supposed to be equal, but I'm the only one to wear a golden circlet on my head. Well, she can have it. I don't want it.

I stare down at the ink. A few words can still be made out on the soaked paper, but it won't be of any use to the new men. I'm beginning to change my opinion on their arrival. It's not exciting, not a happy occasion. No, it's going to end up in a lot of pain and trouble for me. They should have stayed where they came from.

The door opens again and this time, heavy footsteps follow the soft sound of Heather's bare feet.

I lower my gaze, not wanting to look at Andros. He's going to be so angry. It's his reputation that I'm ruining by not having the books ready for the new men. He told everyone they were going to have them tonight. Now, only two will have theirs, if Heather manages to finish hers on time.

"Leave us," he tells the other woman and she hurries away, the door closing behind her with a threatening crack.

He's not saying anything, and I keep my eyes fixed on the floor. There's a pool of ink gathering around one of the table's legs, forming a little blue lake. Andros took me swimming to a lake once, when we'd only just met. He'd surprised me by going in naked, but I found his lack of any kind of embarrassment endearing.

Without warning, his hand lands on my left cheek and my head is thrown to the side. It takes a moment for the pain to reach my brain, but then it's intense. Tears sting in my eyes, running over the sore skin of my cheek. Another slap, my right side this time.

He hits me again and again while I stay standing in my place, not daring to move. It will only make things worse, I've learned that the hard way.

When my head is spinning and I need to grip the back of the chair beside me to keep me from falling, he stops. My cheeks are swollen already, making it hard to keep my eyes open.

I sense him coming closer and prepare for the next slap, but he doesn't do anything. Is he looking at his handiwork? Is he admiring the bruises that are likely beginning to form?

My legs are beginning to shake, but I stay upright. I can't show weakness, he doesn't like that. As soon as he's gone, I can collapse to the floor and let the pain overtake me, but not yet. I just have to hold on a little while longer.

"Take off your robe," he finally says, his voice toneless, passive. He's not showing any emotion, so I will aim to do the same. This isn't personal. It's just a punishment he has to do for the Angel. He's helping me become a better believer.

It wasn't my mistake, it wasn't me who toppled the glass and ruined my work, but maybe if I had been nicer to Heather, if I'd tried to befriend her more, she wouldn't have done it.

He's right to punish me.

I do as he asks, wincing at the movement. I'm not wearing anything beneath the robe and am acutely aware of my nakedness. There is nothing between him and me, no barrier to keep his eyes from devouring me. Is he going to take me again?

Something cold touches my chest. His fingers are wet. I force open my eyes and look down to see what he's doing.

He's writing on my bare chest with the same ink that is covering the table.

Six letters, bright blue on my pale skin.

SINNER.

That hurts me more than the pain in my cheeks.

I'm not a sinner. I'm a follower of the Angel, I'm one of his chosen few. I follow all the rules, I pray, I believe.

I'm not a sinner.

"Go back to your house and wait for me," he tells me, and just to make sure that I know what he means, he picks up my robe from the floor. I'm not going to get it back. He wants me to go back naked, so that everyone can see the words on my chest.

He wants them all to know.

"Please..." I begin, but I stop as soon as he slaps my cheek again. Arguing with him is fruitless.

I take a deep breath and step outside, hoping that there won't be many people around to see me like that.

Of course, I'm not that lucky. There's far more activity out there than normally; preparations for tonight's rituals are involving most members of the community.

They look and stare, but nobody says a word. My skin is on fire with pain and embarrassment and I run across the square towards my own little hut. Tears are blocking my vision, but I know the way by heart.

Just when I think I've left everyone behind, I crash into a hard body and almost fall back, but he grabs me just in time and hold me upright.

"What the..."

I look up, straight into bright blue eyes hidden underneath a red robe. One of the new men. There are little specks of silver in his eyes, making them lighter than their azure blue really is.

"Are you alright?"

His voice rings in my ears and I rip my gaze away from his mesmerizing eyes, back to the safety of the ground. I can feel him stare at me, but all I look at are his bare feet looking out from under the robe.

That's when I remember that I'm naked. No wonder he's staring at me. I step back hastily and he lets me go.

Without looking at him again, I run, reaching my hut in a few steps.

Only when the door has completely closed behind me, I sink to the floor, hugging my legs to my chest, and cry.

Three

He didn't come to me last night. Maybe the Angel took mercy on me and gave him the desire to sleep with one of the community's other women.

The letters on my chest are still just as bright and blue as they were last night. I tried washing them off with a cloth and some soap last night, but it didn't work. They're etched into my skin, a reminder of what Andros thinks of me.

Luckily, today is shower day. Maybe the Angel really is smiling on me for once. Hopefully, the wounds on my back are healed enough not to burst open in the shower. I don't want to stain yet another set of clothing. Blood is hard to get out of fabric, especially with the tools we have at our disposal. I probably generate the most laundry out of everyone, with the exception of the babies. There are two at the moment, Daliah and Revelation, and there's another one on the way.

They're all the Prophet's. The Angel hasn't allowed me a baby yet, so Andros has needed to go to other women to spread his seed. Once we're ready to ascend, one woman and one man will be chosen to stay behind, raise the children until they're old enough to ascend themselves. They will help grow the community further, maybe become the new Prophets. Andros is planning long term, and he doesn't want us to be the last disciples of the Angel.

No, we're only the first generation. He's been spending his time writing down all the Angel's messages, creating his own scriptures. He says that the version we're currently using is only a small part of what the Angel has been telling him. Some things are too sacred for him to share with us, as we wouldn't understand them until we're ready to ascend. Others are aimed at people not living in the community, nonbelievers who haven't heard the message yet. One day, Andros says, everyone will know about the Angel. Once we've ascended, people will be shown what the Angel is promising.

A knock on the door makes me flinch.

"Come in!" I shout weakly, but nobody comes. Intrigued, I cross the room and open the door. A small bundle is sitting on the doorstep, draped in sackcloth.

I take it inside and unwrap it. A note falls to the floor and I pick it up. It's Andros's neat, flourished handwriting.

Wear this today. Be clean for later.

My hands begin to shake and I drop the paper to the floor. The cloth isn't the wrapping. It's what I'm supposed to wear. I unfold it and stare at the sack, three holes cut into it for my head and arms.

There's blood red writing on the front, the same as on my chest.

My eyes sting at the humiliation. Wasn't yesterday enough punishment? Nobody else has ever had to run across the compound naked before. And now I have to wear a sack? It will leave my arms and legs exposed; something we aren't usually allowed. We need to keep our bodies covered. But this...

I sink to the floor, throwing the sack away from me. What am I going to do? I can't resist, I can't defy the Prophet. He's the Angel's voice here on Earth. Sometimes though, I wonder if some of what Andros does isn't actually what the Angel commands. If it's just to satisfy his own desires.

Blasphemy.

I erase the thought from my mind.

If I don't wear it, he will punish me. His wrath will be terrible. He might even turn it into a public punishment, something he only does in extreme cases. I've only been publicly punished once, when I was given the bracelet burned into my ankle.

Others have been punished far more often. I think of Daffodil, rebellious Daffodil who joined the community because her parents did. In the end, she had...

No, don't think of her. Daffodil is gone. No use thinking of the dead.

I stare at the sack. It's not very long, and even though I'm not tall, it will only just cover my upper thighs. If I lean forward, I'll be exposed.

I wipe away my tears and walk to my small cupboard. I don't have many clothes, and they're all of the same style.

Before we moved to the community, I used to wear colourful things, but now everything is white and beige.

Even my underwear is all white. I choose the thickest pair of cotton panties and a bra that's far too big for me. I pair them with knee high white socks. The rule is not to wear shoes, but there's nothing in there about not wearing socks outside. They'll get dirty but right now, I don't care.

The sack cloth is scratchy on my skin, especially where Andros cut holes in it. I'll likely have a rash tonight.

I decide to skip breakfast and head straight to the office. Hopefully, there won't be many people outside and Heather will be the only one to make fun of me.

For once, I'm lucky. Now that the new men have been initiated, everyone is back to doing their normal duties, taking them away from the main square I have to cross.

I hurry to the office building, sighing in relief once the door behind me is closed.

"What on Earth are you wearing?" Heather greets me, her mouth falling open. Her eyes run over my dirty socks, my bare legs and end up hovering over the six red letters on my chest.

I don't reply and sit down at my desk beside her. There's a new stack of fresh paper waiting for me, as well as a copy of the scriptures.

While I begin my task, copying page after page by hand, Heather continues to stare at me, her expression filled with glee. She knows exactly that this is her doing, and she seems to enjoy it. I'm never going to leave my papers lie openly on the table again. She won't get another chance to ruin my work.

I concentrate on the text in the first chapter, the story

of how the Angel first spoke to Andros. My husband was meditating, like he did every day, when a blinding light filled both the room and his mind, transporting him into a white, bare room with walls that glowed. There, the Angel was waiting for him and told him that he was the very first Prophet, the man chosen to spread the Angel's message. At first, Andros was unconvinced, but the Angel showed him both the extent of his power and a glimpse of Paradise and the Prophet started to believe.

The day after this first vision, he began to tell others about his experience and soon amassed a group of followers. I was one of them, and I soon became more than just one of Andros's flock. First I turned into his lover, then soon after, his wife.

He was very different back then.

"Stop daydreaming and work." Heather's harsh voice pulls me back to my task and I continue my writing. I'm slower than yesterday though, and by the time the midday bell rings, I've only got about a quarter of the book done. My skin is itching all over from the scratchy cloth I'm wearing, but it's yet another few hours until shower time.

The sky outside is grey, but sadly it's not raining. If it was, we'd assemble in the hall where I could sneak in last and kneel at the back where not as many people would see me. Instead, I'll have to stand in a circle outside, in full view of the entire community. A blush rises up my cheeks.

I'll have to get through this.

"Angel be with me," I whisper quietly enough for Heather not to hear. She's almost out of the door already, shooting me a suspicious glance as if she knows that I'm debating whether to go to the prayer.

No, the punishment for that would be too severe. I need to attend.

I take a deep breath and recite the Angel's words in my head.

Discipline leads to redemption.
Suffering brings peace.

Focussing on the mantra, I step outside, keeping my eyes fixed on the ground. With every step I get closer to the statue, the temptation to run away increases. Not just to my house. No, away from the compound, away from Andros.

Obedience inspires happiness.

Maybe this humiliation will bring happiness, too. Maybe it'll make me a better person. Maybe it's all just a test by the Angel to see who his most loyal believers are.

I breathe in deep. Yes, I am loyal. I believe in the Angel with all my heart. I may not like Andros, but I love the Angel. For him, it's all worth it.

That thought gives me new strength and I manage to take the final steps, taking my place in the circle. I don't know who I'm standing next to, but I don't dare look up and see all their stares.

"Laya!" Andros's booming voice shatters through the confidence I just gathered and breaks me into a million frightened pieces. Run, the voice in my head screams, but I can't. I have to stay. The pain in my ankle flares up and reminds me that running away isn't an option.

"Come here!"

Before I can even think, my feet follow his command, carrying me to the centre of the circle. I stop when I'm in front of him, his bare feet all I can see of him. I don't want to look up, but he takes that decision away from me by putting a finger underneath my chin and lifting my head.

"Look me in the eyes," he orders.

I don't comply, fixing my gaze on his mouth instead. His lips are beautifully curved, the colour so red it almost looks like he's wearing lipstick. I used to love his lips, especially when he kissed me.

The times of gentle, sensuous kisses are over. Have been, for a long time.

Andros doesn't insist on me meeting his eyes and grabs my shoulders instead, turning me around until I look at the assembled crowd. Now they can all see me. The words on my tunic. The proof of my sin.

There are no whispers, they are too obedient for that, but I can almost feel their thoughts as they're wondering what I've done to be treated in this way.

"My wife made a grievous mistake yesterday," Andros announces, his voice too loud in my ears. "Tell them what you did, Laya."

I don't know what to say. It was Heather who drenched the pages, not me. I didn't do anything. But I can't tell him that. He'll just punish me even more.

Andros takes my hesitation as defiance and slaps me from behind, his fingernails grazing my cheek because of the awkward angle. I flinch but his grip on me is too strong to move.

"My Princess defiled the Angel's words!" he shouts, anger brimming in his voice, making me shudder in fear.

"She poured water on the words that I myself wrote. I wouldn't have needed to share the Angel's message, I could have kept his wisdom and guidance for myself. But did I? No! I shared it, I wrote it down so you all could read it and follow the Angel. But Laya, my wife, my Princess, she damaged the words!"

Spittle hits my neck as he roars the last words.

How did I ever love this man?

"Are you sorry for what you've done?"

I didn't do anything, so how can I be sorry for it?

Still, there's no other way. "Yes," I whisper.

"Louder! Tell them all."

I lift my voice. "I'm sorry."

"Will you do it again?"

I shake my head. "No, Prophet."

His grip on my shoulders tightens. What more is he going to do? Isn't this enough?

"Will you accept your punishment?"

His voice is a snarl now with an edge of barely disguised excitement. He's looking forward to punishing me further. I was wrong, making me run naked and dressing me in a sack wasn't the punishment. It was only the foreplay to something much, much worse.

His fingers are digging into my shoulders and he begins to shake me.

"Do you accept your punishment?"

I squeeze my eyes shut, preparing for whatever he's about to do.

"Yes." It's barely a whisper, but it's enough for him.

He turns me around and presses me against the large pedestal the statue of the Angel is resting on.

"Look at the Angel," he instructs. "Look at the Angel and ask for forgiveness."

He lifts the sackcloth and rips down my panties, exposing me to the crowd. I whimper as I hear his zipper. This isn't just going to be a public beating. I grip the pole tightly, my shaking legs barely supporting me. I feel him against my entrance and I press my legs together, but all that earns me is a hard slap on my cheeks.

"Spread your legs."

He hits me again to emphasize, and I do as he asks. There's no other way. He steps in between my legs and grips my hips, roughly shoving me against him.

Then he takes me, in front of everyone, grunting like an animal as he pounds into me. I keep my eyes fixed on the Angel like he instructed, blinking through the tears.

Angel, please help me. Please, if you're listening, help me. Let me ascend now and be at your side. Don't make me wait and stay on this world with him.

Four

I don't bother getting up when someone enters my room. I've been staring at the ceiling for the past few hours, refusing to move my aching body. Andros's public punishment yesterday afternoon had been only the beginning. After some of the women had helped me shower, he'd returned in the evening to leave new marks on my skin.

I can feel the blood seep into the sheets beneath me, but I don't care. Those stains can be removed. The ones on my soul are permanent.

Why is the Angel letting this happen? Is he not watching over us like Andros says? Are there other followers he's occupied with instead? Are we not worthy of his attention?

A plate is carelessly dumped next to me and a moment later, I'm alone again. The smell of freshly baked bread makes me turn my head. A perfectly formed roll sits on the plate, a thick layer of butter gluing the two halves together.

Nobody has ever brought me breakfast before. Missing meal times means going hungry. Not today, it seems.

My stomach painfully reminds me how hungry I am, and I sit up, groaning in pain. Some of the wounds must be deep.

The roll looks delicious, much better than our usual boring food. Meals are just for sustenance, not enjoyment, that's one of the Angel's messages. We're only here on Earth temporarily, and while we need to keep care of our bodies, we don't need to indulge.

I breathe in the scent, wanting to prolong the experience as much as possible, before taking the first bite. It tastes just as wonderful as it smells. I take another bite – and hit something hard. I lower the roll and open the two halves. There's a piece of paper in there, folded up several times.

I frown, confused. Connor is the man usually cooking for us, and I've never really talked to him. He doesn't say much and all our conversations have revolved around food. Why would he send me a message in this way?

I unfold the paper and my eyes widen.

You'll be safe soon. Hold on.

I read the message several times before crumpling the paper in my fist. Is this another test?

Safe. Soon.

But I am safe. I'm in the Angel's community. There's no better place to live.

Hold on.

For what? Till when? What's going to happen? My thoughts are racing, but I know there aren't any answers to be found. I don't know enough. I can't come to conclusions with this tiny amount of information.

This must be a test. Does Andros want me to give this note to him to show that I don't keep secrets from the community? Or should I confess to the Angel?

My head hurts from all the consequences this note could have. I unfold it and read it again. And again.

For some reason, it gives me hope, even if it is just a test.

I fold the paper carefully this time, making it as small as I can, and then stuff it in between the floor boards beneath my mattress. I have an old photograph of my parents in there too. We're not supposed to have anything reminding us of our old lives, but I couldn't throw this picture away. I resist looking at it now; the gentle smile of my mother and the contemplative glance of my father are burned into my mind already.

My father is dead, he died of a heart attack shortly after I'd joined Andros and the community. My mother sent word, but Andros didn't want me to go to the funeral. Too emotional, he said. Instead, we sat and prayed to the Angel, hoping that he would allow my father into his realm of peace and eternal light.

I'm not sure where my mother is, or if she's still alive. There are no other close relatives who would get in touch with me should something happen to her.

She's not one of the Angel's flock, though. She didn't want to join us, no matter how much I begged her. I'll likely never see her again, whether in this life or the next.

The community is my family now.

I don't get up when the midday bell rings. It will be the first time I miss prayer since I was ill with the flu a few months ago and couldn't leave my bed for days.

My back aches with every movement, so I'm lying on my stomach, arms outstretched, my head bent to one side. It's the most comfortable position, despite the strain on my neck muscles.

Blood is still seeping from my wounds, but I've taken off my shirt so that my clothes don't get stained any further. A cool breeze caresses my back, making me grateful that I left the window open. I turn my head to look out into the sunshine. It's sunny but cold, as it is so often in the Scottish summer. Unless it's raining, of course. Here in the Highlands the weather can change in an instant.

The sun is too high in the sky right now to shine into my house, but I still enjoy its light. It reminds me of the Angel's glow that Andros describes in his scriptures. Like sunlight reflected by morning dew, it says in his book. Despite his dark side, Andros is a poet at heart, an artist. He used to paint when I got to know him, but he stopped when he founded this community. There is no time for idle pastimes like that. It doesn't help in getting us closer to ascension.

I close my eyes, ready to dream of the light of the Angel, when something hits the ground next to me and I shriek, turning and wrapping my sheets around me like a shield.

I look around, panicked, but there is nobody there. What just happened?

Oh.

There's a small brown parcel on the floor below the window; someone must have thrown it in. Hesitantly, I take and unwrap it. It's an apple, red and juicy, with one word scratched into the peel:

Soon.

I grip it tightly, tempted to throw the apple away from me. Is that a threat? A promise? Something else?

But then my stomach growls and I take a bite, erasing the confusing message from the apple. It's sweet and tangy at the same time and a trickle of juice runs down my chin as I eat hungrily. This is turning into a day full of food that I wouldn't usually get.

I eat the entire apple, including the seeds, to make sure that nobody will find any trace of it. This wasn't one of our homegrown, small apples, this was one that was bought somewhere. Who could have brought this to our community? The only person who has contact with the outside world is Andros. So it is a test.

But wait, the three new men. They could have brought the apple in their bags when they arrived. But why would they break the rules? Why would they give me an apple? We've never even spoken, and we likely never will. Women don't talk to men, especially not me, the Princess, the Prophet's wife.

The hazy memory of me running into one of them flashes through my mind, but I push it away. I don't want to be remembered of that humiliation.

I fold the brown paper, but wait, there's something else hidden in the parcel. A small tube, no longer than my little finger. Antiseptic cream, it says on the label.

A shiver runs over my skin. While the apple may have been a grey zone, this is definitely forbidden. We're not allowed to use creams and medicine. If the Angel wants us to suffer, we suffer. We're not supposed to ease our pain with manmade substances.

I roll the tube in between my fingers, debating what to do. My back hurts and I'm sure this cream would help with the pain and the risk of infection, but is it worth the risk?

Petal could come any moment to help me wash my back, or Andros himself could show up demanding to know why I wasn't at the prayer. And the Angel doesn't allow it in any case.

This is a test.

Pain is salvation.

I take the little tube and push it into my hiding place. If I throw it away, someone might find it in the rubbish. I could bury it, but something stops me from destroying this tiny trace of hope. The hope that there's someone out there who cares about me, who wants to stop my pain.

It's probably a foolish notion, but I can't help but feel hopeful. Maybe things will change.

I smile and lie back down, exposing my back once again to the cool air. I won't be using the cream, but the knowledge that it's there, under my mattress, is making me feel better already.

Five

Andros left me alone for two days, but last night, he came to my room and forced himself on me, whispering how much he was enjoying being with his 'little bird', how the other women weren't able to satisfy him as much as I do.

I wish it wasn't this way. I've not returned his kisses, his touches, but still he feels like I'm wanting his attention. Sometimes I want to scream and fight, but I've done that in the past and have learned that it only makes things worse. If I resist, he will punish me, and that pain lasts much longer than the sharp ache between my legs when he enters me roughly.

He didn't leave last night after he had spent himself inside me, telling me that he hoped this would finally be the time he got me pregnant. He's still here, his arm wrapped around me like a shackle.

"I'm sorry I had to punish you," he suddenly whispers and I freeze. I hadn't realised he was awake. "It's what the Angel demands, you understand? I wouldn't hurt you if I didn't have to. But the Angel demands discipline and we all have to follow his rules, especially the two of us. We're examples to the community and we can't be seen to bend his commandments. You understand that, right?"

His arm around me tightens and I stop breathing, anxiously waiting what he's going to do next. Is he going to hurt me again?

"Do you understand?" His voice has turned harsher, with an underlying desperation. I realise he wants absolution. He wants me to confirm that it's not Andros's fault. He knows what he's doing isn't right, but if he can find a reason for it, he won't have to feel guilty for it.

I wish I could give him absolution.

I wish I was strong enough to lie.

But I can't.

"No," I whisper, cringing as I seal my fate. "It's you, not the Angel."

I wait for the coming explosion, but Andros doesn't say anything. He's quiet, letting me quiver in fear of what's to come. He's always been a master of the dreaded silence, that moment when the entire world is about to crumble and he alone can make it stop by saying something. By disturbing the silence that he himself has created.

He takes his arm off my waist, stopping the painful embrace, and rolls away from me. Is he going to leave?

I don't dare move, so I stay in the same position, suppressing the anxious whimper that is threatening to burst from my chest. I won't give him the satisfaction. I'm going to stay quiet, no matter what he does to me. When I cry or beg, it just gets worse.

The blanket that was covering both of us is pulled back,

exposing my naked body to the dim light of the dawn streaming through the dirty windows.

"Lie on your back," Andros suddenly says quietly. His quiet voice is the worst. It's a warning, a threat that he's about to do some terrible things to me.

The urge to jump up and run burns through me, but as always, pain shoots through my ankle where the bracelet is fused to my skin. I know the pain is just in my mind, but that doesn't make it any less agonising. I'm trapped, at the mercy of the Prophet, and he knows it.

I turn and look up at him. A cruel smile is twisting his lips, but his eyes are cold, staring down at me as if I'm nothing but dirt under his fingernails. Maybe that's what I am. Not worthy of him, the man who has spoken to the Angel, who is ready for ascension.

I close my eyes and wait for whatever is to come.

"Look at me," he orders and hesitantly, I do as he asks. He runs a finger over my cheek, then lower until he reaches my lips. Once, I would have thought this a gentle gesture but right now it's possessive and foreboding.

"Keep your eyes on mine," he warns, and there's no doubt that he will punish me if I don't do as he says. I look at him, but not in his eyes, I can't bear to see the cruelty in them. I focus on his eyebrows instead, his smooth forehead, the tiny scar just below the hairline.

His fingers trail even lower until his hand is on my throat. He gently strokes my skin there, then, without warning, he's on top of me, sitting on my hips, both his hands around my throat.

I struggle, trying to sit up, but he's too strong. His thumbs press against my thorax and his grip tightens, cutting off my air supply. I try to breathe, gasp for air, but it's no use. He's strangling me and there's nothing I can do. I reach for him, my fingers almost touching his face, but he just leans back and laughs at my feeble attempts to get him off me. I grasp his hands, squeezing my fingernails into his flesh, but already dark spots are dancing before my eyes and I can feel all strength leave my weak body.

"It's the Angel's command," he tells me calmly. "He doesn't want you to disobey him."

I want to tell him that the Angel would never want him to choke someone, but pain and darkness overwhelm me, taking me into their gentle arms and carrying me far, far away.

Life flows back into me, slowly, painfully. I'm almost disappointed. Death seems like the only escape I have and even that Andros is refusing me. He must have stopped once I was unconscious. I sit up with a groan which hurts my throat. I'm aching all over, not just my neck. There's wetness between my legs. I run a finger over my skin there and it's covered in blood when I look at it. What did he do to me? He must have been incredibly rough. There's a pain deep inside of me, a dumb ache that makes me suspect that he injured me somehow. He's made me bleed before, but this is different. I grab a towel and press it between my legs, soaking up the blood. Hopefully it'll stop soon so I can go outside and... and do what, exactly? Am I expected to go back to the office and work there?

Or does he want me to stay here to punish me some more?

I gingerly touch my throat. It's sore and swollen. I bet there's bruising, but I don't have a mirror to check. Usually, we're only allowed to wear scarves in winter, but I'll break that rule today. Maybe he'll even approve; I don't know if Andros wants everyone to know what he did to me. He always keeps the bruises to places people can't see. The women who help clean me up after his whippings are the only ones who see the extent of his violence. Well, until he took me in public. I'm sure everyone saw the scars on my back then. I shudder in a mixture of fear and anger. The past months have been nothing but pain. He's been getting worse and instead of weekly beatings, they've become almost daily. Sometimes even more than once a day. My wounds no longer have time to heal. He'll kill me soon if he continues like it. Maybe he doesn't care. Maybe that's what he wants. Destroy me bit by bit, until I'm nothing more than a shell that he can crumble into dust.

I won't let that happen. I may not fight him, but that's not because I give up. It's because I'm saving my strength for the time I will be able to leave.

I ignore the pain in my ankle. Yes, I will leave. Somehow.

Even if it's in a coffin. I can't stay here any longer. The pain in my throat and my belly are proof of that. I can serve the Angel in other places, even if I'll never reach ascension. Maybe the Angel will have mercy with me and talk to me, tell me how to be saved.

I see it now. I can still be one of the children of the Angel even if I'm not with Andros.

Leave. I will leave.

Six

Nobody comes to clean me up. Nobody tells me to go to work. Around midday, an apple is thrown through my window, but I'm too sore to get up in time to see who threw it in. There are two letters and a question mark scratched into the peel.

OK?

No, I'm not. But how am I supposed to tell that my mystery messenger? If this is a trap, any reaction to it would be dangerous.

I nibble on the apple, but my throat hurts when I try to swallow. I hide it under my blankets for later.

Blood is still seeping into the towel between my legs. The pain is getting worse and a dumb throbbing has started to tear through my lower body. I curl up on my side, which is the least painful way of lying down. All I can do is wait, either for the bleeding to stop, or for it to get so bad that I'll bleed out. Maybe that wouldn't be so bad.

. . .

I don't open my eyes when the door opens. It's too difficult. I stay in my curled up position, cradling the pain within me, holding it close. If I let it go, I'll break apart.

"Laya?"

A cool hand touches my forehead. It's a woman, but I don't recognise her. The fog in my brain doesn't let me access my memories.

Footsteps go, then come, then go again.

The door opens several times and there are voices all around me.

I ignore them, floating away on my cloud of pain.

Someone touches my ankles and I whimper, expecting Andros to finish what he started. I can remember him, even if I can't remember others. He's all that fills my mind, his dark eyes, his discipline, his pain.

"Shhh, I'm a doctor."

The voice isn't Andros, that's all I know.

I struggle weakly against the grip, but I'm like a moth fighting an elephant. I have no chance.

My body is moved until I'm lying on my back and my legs are spread. Pain shoots through me and I'm ripped apart.

I scream, but no sound leaves my throat.

His voice runs through my dreams.

"I'm a doctor."

A doctor is someone who heals, saves, helps.

He says other things too, and I'm not sure if they're a

dream or real, but they make me feel safe. I stay in my dream world for a long time, refusing to wake up.

In my dreams, his voice is comforting me.

When I wake up, he may not be there. Maybe he's not even real. Maybe all that awaits me is Andros and more pain.

Eventually though, I can't stay asleep any longer.

As much as I want to avoid the reality of life, my brain refuses to stay unconscious. I leave the safety of my dream world and step back into my body.

"I think she's waking up."

A woman, familiar. Rose. Pretty, lovely Rose, married to Bryan, someone as wild as she is delicate.

"Laya?"

She touches my cheek, just below my left eye, and I blink.

"You can leave now," she says, confusing me. She wants me to leave? I don't think I can. I try moving my arms but they're too heavy.

"I'll need to do some tests first," a deep voice says. I recognise it immediately. 'I'm a doctor' echoes through my mind. He's real. I didn't imagine him.

"Be quick about it." Rose sounds harsh and shrill and I turn away from her voice. I want the doctor, not her. "The Prophet won't like you being alone with her."

"Well, that's why she has you as her chaperone," he replies calmly. "The Prophet told me to make her better, so that's what I'm doing."

A hand embraces my wrist, probably feeling my pulse.

"Laya, open your eyes," he says softly, his voice caressing me, lulling me into the belief that everything will be alright. That I'll be safe.

I do as he asked. Slowly, his face comes into focus. His red robe is the first thing I see. He's one of the new men. A shadow of a beard covers his cheeks. I want to tell him that he'll have to shave it, but my voice isn't cooperating. I don't want him to be punished. All men have to be clean shaven and have short hair, that's the rule, just like all women have to have their hair shorn every two weeks.

He looks into my eyes, gently lifting my eyelids one after the other.

"Don't speak," he tells me, oblivious that I don't have the strength to do so. "You'll have to stay quiet for at least a day or two, so your throat can recover. Don't get up either. Rose here will get you soup and water. I've managed to stop the bleeding, but without proper tools or medication there's not much else I can do. Try to move as little as possible, and use the bedpan, don't get up for that. I'll come back to check on you soon."

He makes it sound like a promise, like something special. I'm not used to people making promises that aren't about hurting me. I think I like it.

Clouds are edging over my vision and my eyes flutter closed.

"Sleep and recover," he says gently. I want to ask him his name, but I'm too far gone. Martin, Noran, Owen. It has to be one of those three.

Martin, Noran, Owen.

Martin, Noran, Owen.

The names become my mantra that lull me to sleep.

Seven

It takes four days until I'm able to get up. Four days of a grumpy Rose feeding me soup and emptying my bedpan. I try and talk to her, but talking hurts and she's not interested anyway. I always thought her to be a gentle and caring woman, but she's treating me with an indifference that makes me re-evaluate my perception of her.

The highlight of my days is when the doctor comes to visit. I still don't know his name.

Martin, Noran, Owen.

Rose is there whenever he comes, and I don't want to ask him in front of her. I don't want her to tell Andros that I asked for the name of the doctor. Us women aren't supposed to talk to the men of the community, unless we absolutely have to or they're our husbands. So all I do is answer his questions about where it hurts and how I'm feeling.

Andros hasn't visited once and I'm incredibly grateful for that. Not that I believe that he does it out of consideration for my wellbeing. No, he can't stand to see his canvas spoilt and dirty. He's waiting until I'm feeling better, and then he's going to come and continue his art.

Until then, he's probably using the other women of the community to satisfy his desires. I don't think he hits any of them, but he certainly sleeps with them.

No, I'm his only canvas, the only one he marks with red stripes.

On the fourth day, Rose leaves with the bedpan, muttering something about how I should be cleaning up my own mess. As soon as she's gone, the door opens again. It's the doctor. He looks over his shoulder as if he's very aware that he shouldn't be alone with me.

In a few large steps, he's by my side.

"We don't have much time," he whispers hurriedly. He hands me some pills and a bottle of water. "I had those smuggled in, so take them now. They're antibiotics and iron tablets. The blood loss has made you anaemic, but Andros wouldn't allow me to get you proper treatment."

For a moment, his frown tells me what he thinks about that, but then his expression smoothens as if he's unaffected by the Prophet's treatment of me, his wife.

"Has he done that before?" he asks quietly.

"Not this bad," I croak, before quickly adding, "But I deserved it."

Even though my heart is telling me that I can trust this man, I've learned to be cautious with everything I say.

He nods brusquely, neither confirming nor denying my statement. He's careful as well. Good. That will keep him safe. He's probably in Andros's bad books for treating me with such care and gentleness, but if he keeps his head down, he'll become a valuable part of the community. We haven't had a doctor for a long time now, and even though we're not allowed to use man-made treatments, it will be good to have him.

I take the tablets, ignoring the feeling of guilt spreading through my stomach. These are going to help me. I need to stay alive to serve the Angel. I can't stay weak and ill.

I pass the bottle of water back to him and he hides it under his dark red robes just in time. Rose doesn't bother knocking, but she stops in the doorframe when she sees the doctor kneeling by my side.

"Why are you here?" she asks him, but it sounds more like an accusation than a question.

"I needed to check on her earlier today because I've got lessons with the Prophet all afternoon," he explains calmly. "She's doing well, maybe she can get up and move around a bit tomorrow."

That brings a smile on Rose's face. She must be thinking of the prospect of not having to empty my bedpans anymore. Well, I'll be happy about that too. It's embarrassing to be so reliant on other people.

"I'll come again tomorrow morning," the doctor promises. "Then we'll see if you're ready."

He gives me a smile, but his eyes are clouded with emotion. Worry? Anger? Fear?

He's so hard to read, especially for a new believer. It usually takes them a while to get used to hiding their thoughts and feelings, but this man is already adept at it.

"I'll accompany you to the Prophet," Rose announces and steps out of the house, leaving the doctor and me alone for one last moment.

"What's your name?" I ask him.

"A- Martin," he corrects himself, using the name the Prophet has given him.

I smile at him and then immediately straighten my expression just in case Rose returns.

"Stay safe," he mutters and leaves.

What a strange thing to say. Shouldn't he believe that this is a safe place? That this is where all the Angel's chosen children live until the ascension? It's the best and safest place there is.

The Angel. I've not prayed to him in days, both because of my pain and the tiredness stopping me from thinking straight.

The Angel is our shield and our refuge.
The Angel is our shield and our refuge.

I repeat the mantra over and over again until sleep takes me once again, letting me drift off to a place of peace.

It's late afternoon by the time I get my next visitor. When the sound of the door opening wakes me, I assume its Rose bringing food, but the footsteps aren't hers. Those are heavy, familiar steps and my heart shudders in fear.

Andros.

He kneels by my side, his knees pressing into my back. I stay curled up on my side, not daring to move.

"How are you, my gentle little bird?"

His voice is sweet and melodic. Once I would have turned around and kissed him. Now, that thought alone makes me want to throw up.

He runs a hand over my side, stopping when he reaches my hipbone. He grips it tight.

"You haven't apologised to me yet," he says quietly, steal lacing his words.

Apologise? What for?

I don't voice that question. It wouldn't do any good.

"I'm sorry," I whisper obediently. Speaking hurts.

"Good girl. What will you do to make it up to me?"

I cringe. He's going to want to use me again. Continue his art on my back. Bury himself in me to forget about his anger.

I know the answer. It's not the first time I've had to say it. "Anything the Angel requires of me."

My voice is barely a whisper, but he seems to have heard it. Instead of answering me like he usually does, he suddenly takes his hand from my hip and slaps my side.

"No. Not what the Angel requires. What I want. You serve me, the Prophet. I'm the Angel's servant, but you are mine. Tell me you're mine. Tell me you'll do whatever I want."

I can't do that. Serving the Angel, I can do. Explaining all his violence as the Angel's will, I can do. But being told that he's doing it just for his own pleasure... it's too much. The glass palace of illusions I'd built up so carefully is beginning to crack.

"I serve the Angel," I croak. "The Angel wouldn't want you to do this to me."

There. I said it. And signed my death warrant at the same time. I close my eyes and await his wrath.

But it doesn't come.

There's just silence. Andros doesn't move. His hand doesn't return to my hip. He's not hitting me. Not calling me names. He's just kneeling there, not saying anything.

My breath is getting quicker. I'm scared of what's about to happen. We're in new territory here. I've never questioned him before. I was never brave enough. I don't know what's changed. He almost killed me; I should be even more frightened of him now. Not defiant.

"You think the Angel doesn't want me to punish you?" he finally asks, his voice soft and almost gentle. "You're wrong. He shows me visions of you every night. In each one of them you're screaming in pain. This is exactly what he wants. You're taking the sins of this community upon yourself. By being punished, you're making sure that the others don't have to suffer the same fate. You're so generous in your pain, sweet little bird. It hurts me to punish you, but we both know that you want it. And so does the Angel. He tells me to do it. I have no choice."

Cold shivers wash over me. The Angel wants it. He wants me to suffer, he's been wanting it all along. It wasn't Andros. Yes, Andros enjoys it, but that's not why he does it. Not just.

The Angel wants me to be punished.

I'm the one to carry all sins.

I should be happy to save others from being punished for their sins.

I should be proud.

Then why am I crying?

Eight

I'm no longer allowed to leave my hut except for midday and evening prayers. For those, Andros himself comes to pick me up and then brings me back to the hut afterwards. He's not letting me talk to anyone. He's not letting the doctor check on me either. Maybe he's scared that Martin will see the new wounds and bruises.

The three new men are still wearing their bright red robes that increasingly make me think of blood. It will take months until they're ready to be initiated and progress to the white robes the rest of us wear for formal occasions.

I now wear mine all the time. Andros has taken away all my normal clothes.

That day when he told me that it was the Angel punishing me, it changed things. He's treating me differently. It's like we're sharing a secret, a mission that puts us above everyone else. I've always been different, the circlet on my head the visible proof for it, but now, the way he keeps me apart from the others separates me even more from the community.

He's put a smaller statue of the Angel into my bedroom and makes me look at it when he whips me. He says I should be grateful to be given such an important role. I am, sometimes, when the pain lets me think. It's always there now, the pain. Before, I had respites, days when he didn't come and break open old wounds. Now, he comes to me daily.

Last night, he entered me several times. He wants me to bear his child, and once the child is born, it will take on all our sins so we can ascend. I don't know what that means, how an infant can take over the role I'm doing right now, but I know that I don't want to bring a baby into this community. I'm hoping that my prayers and determination will stop me from conceiving.

The only things that keep me from going insane are the gifts that continue to reach me in one way or another. It's mostly food; apples thrown through the window, sweets hidden in dry bread rolls, even a piece of chocolate wrapped in a towel. Whoever is giving me these things hasn't given up. There are no more messages, no more promises, but the simple existence of the gifts gives me hope.

Nothing new happens for a month. Life goes on. Prayers twice a day, copying the Angel's messages in between meals, and visits from Andros in the evening. Sometimes, in the morning, he tells me what the Angel showed him in his dreams and makes me write it all down. A lot of it is about me, and the sins I'm suffering for.

Jeremy had heretic thoughts. Laya needs to be beaten.

Jasmine was late for prayer. Laya needs to be whipped.

Bryan broke a plate. Laya needs to be kicked.

The monotony of it is almost soothing. Every day is the same and only the mode of punishment changes. Andros systematically works his way up and down my body, letting the wounds heal just enough to be able to place new ones on top. It's a miracle that I haven't died of infections yet. He doesn't let the women come in to clean me anymore. I have to do it myself, twisting in pain so I can wipe the dried blood of my back.

But now, after his talks of a baby last night, I feel that things are about to change. It makes me scared. I can deal with the present. It's become predictable. I can prepare for what's going to happen, and that makes it more bearable.

"The Angel showed me how to prepare you all for ascension," Andros says suddenly. He's hugging me from behind, his sweaty body touching mine. He stayed last night, which means I didn't get any sleep. His presence keeps me from being able to drift off.

"It's almost time."

My heart begins to beat faster. Ascension! That means leaving the confines of this world and joining the Angel in Paradise. The pain will be over.

"When?" I ask quickly before I can stop myself.

"Soon. I need to start making preparations. Ascending on my own is easy, but to take you all with me, I need to get more guidance from the Angel." He kisses my neck and I manage not to pull back. "You will finally be able to fly, little bird. We will fly into Paradise together to sit by the Angel's side."

I smile, for the first time in weeks.

"I'm ready," I tell Andros, and turn to look at the Angel statue above us, looking down on us in all his glory.

It turns out that Andros needs supplies for the ascension that we don't have in the compound, so he leaves for a few days. It's been a long time since he last did that, and the mood in the community is anxious, hesitant. We're insecure without our Prophet, and nobody is confident enough to take charge, not even Eamon, who Andros named his deputy while he's away.

Strangely enough, I miss him. I miss his visits, even the pain that he gives me. What's happening to the sins while he's not passing them on to me? Will this mean that our community's ascension will be delayed? I'm tempted to punish myself, take the whip and splash it across my back like Andros does, but I don't know the sins of our people. Andros does, he dreams of them or they come and confess to him, so I need to wait for him.

At the first midday prayer without Andros, I stand among the others, not in the centre with the Prophet. It's a strange feeling to be back in their midst, but I don't mind it. Even Heather's hate-filled stare doesn't bother me. We're close to ascension, that's all that matters.

The Angel is our shield and our refuge.

I chant as loud as I can, my voice lifting to the heavens. We are the children of the Angel and he will welcome us with open arms, that's what has been foretold.

After prayer, I head back to my house like I'm used to.

There are several books waiting to be copied, and I want to be done with them by the time Andros returns. Just before I reach my hut, someone steps into my path. He's wearing the red robe of the new followers, but it's not the doctor. Instead of Martin's moss green gaze, silver blue eyes capture mine. It's the same man I stumbled into when I had to run naked across the square. I blush at the memory.

His hair is shorn close to his scalp, but its striking white-blond colour is still obvious. It's like he's wearing a halo.

"Apologies," he mutters, breaking eye contact and looking at the ground. "Your husband gave me a task but I'm having trouble completing it. I was wondering if you might be able to help me."

I want to say no, that he'll have to wait until Andros is back, that it's not proper for me to be with an unmarried man, a novice at that. But then he lifts his eyes again and I can't help but nod.

"How can I help?"

From the corner of my eyes, I see Eamon approaching us, a mixture of curiosity and apprehension on his face. "It's alright," I call to him, "the Prophet sent him."

Eamon gives me a sharp look, but then nods and walks away, leaving me alone with the man. I don't even know his name. He could be either Noran or Owen, but it would be impolite to ask.

"Can we go inside?" he asks, pointing towards my house. It only really consists of one large room, which is split into a living and sleeping area. There's a small bathroom with a toilet and a sink as well, but the tap doesn't always work and we shower in the communal wash house anyway. I think of the bloody towels and the angel statue above my dirty mattress, and decide that I don't want him to see that. He's still new and probably wouldn't understand it.

"Let's talk here," I say quickly, turning so my body is blocking the way to my door. "How can I help?"

He takes a book from beneath his robe. It's the book, the Angel's words.

"I've been reading the chapters the Prophet assigned us, but I have a few questions that make it difficult for me to continue without knowing the answers. I thought that you, as the Prophet's wife, might be able to explain?"

He's right. I know the scriptures better than anyone - Andros excluded - both from copying them dozens of times and from listening to Andros telling me about his visions. Back when we first met, he told me of his dreams and it was me who urged him to write them down. I know most of the book by heart.

"Which chapters are you referring to?" I ask, but before he answers, I suggest, "Let's go to the office. There are other books there that I might be able to give you for further reading."

He follows me to the community buildings. I haven't been in the office for weeks now; my work has been brought to my house. It feels strange to be back.

I knock on the door, expecting Heather to open, but she doesn't seem to be back from lunch yet.

I let the man go in first and look around, checking if anyone saw us go in. It's strange, I feel guilty about doing this, even though it's nothing forbidden. On the contrary, I'm helping someone learn more about the Angel's message, so that should be encouraged, right? Yes, I'm alone with a man, but we're in a public building and not in my house. This should be fine.

I take a seat at my old desk while the man has already sat down on a bench by the window. He opens the book towards the end, and points at a page that is full of notes and underlined passages. He really has been studying the Prophet's words.

"In chapter nineteen, it speaks of ascension, and how it's the only way we can be with the Angel. Does that mean people dying of old age won't get to be with the Angel, even if they've been his followers all their life?"

I smile. I feel needed for the first time in ages. Copying the scriptures is a necessary task and I don't mind doing it, but this is far more interesting.

"That depends on the Angel's decision," I explain. "Everybody who reaches ascension is automatically allowed into the Angel's Paradise. Those who don't will have to bow to his judgement. Of course, those who have served him before they died will be treated more favourably. That he promises."

The man nods, apparently satisfied by my explanation. He flicks a few pages further and shows me the paragraph he's underlined.

"And the Angel told me that a great plague was to come, and he warned me that I should gather my followers and move into the wilderness to be safe from the poison infecting humanity's hearts. For this was a plague of the mind and the heart, not of the body. He then told me that the only way to escape the suffering of the human condition is by ascending to his side, gathering the courage to end our mortal existence and join the Angel in his glorious Paradise."

I recite the words without having to read them. They're embedded into my heart, burned into every fibre of my being.

"The thing I don't quite understand," the novice says, pointing at the final sentence, "is the bit about ending our mortal existence. How does that happen? Isn't that the same as dying?"

Andros should be the one to explain. He's the one who introduces the concept of Ascension to the new believers, not me. It's a bit too early as well. Their trust in the Angel needs to be built up first, layer upon layer, before we can tell them what their path of salvation entails.

"No, it's not dying," I explain with a smile. "It's leaving our earthly shell and joining with the Angel. Dying is final. Ascension isn't."

"But..." He frowns, staring at the book. "But we're leaving this world, right? So it's like dying?"

"Is flying with wings and flying on a plane the same thing?" I ask in return.

He shakes his head.

"See? It's the same with ascension. Death is like stepping onto a plane, letting someone else do the work, passively moving through the air. Flying yourself like a bird, using your wings, deciding to explore the skies of your own volition, that's different. Ascension is a conscious process. We're not waiting for death to take us. We're taking flight on our own, so to speak, to reach the Angel."

He looks as if he wants to ask me more, but he keeps his eyes on the book, the cogs in his head clearly working hard.

I feel like I need to reassure him, tell him that it's not what he thinks it is.

"Andros has seen our future," I say softly. "The Angel speaks to him. We'll be safe and happy by the Angel's side. We'll want for nothing and we'll be basking in his glory for eternity. Don't worry. It will all become clearer the more of the scriptures you read. When the Prophet is back, he will be able to pray with you."

"Thank you." He bows his head in deference. "I should let you return to your work. But... can I come back if I have further questions? You've helped me a lot."

A warmth settles in me, an unfamiliar feeling. "Of course," I stutter, taken aback by how thankful he seems to be. "While my husband isn't here, I'll do my best to help you understand the Angel's message."

He smiles at me, his eyes sparkling, and leaves. His smile stays in my mind, an echo of a conversation we shouldn't have had. Not because of what we said, but because I was alone with him, a man, without a chaperone.

Nine

On the second day of Andros's absence, I'm holed up in my house again, waiting for the midday prayer bell. It's probably going to be another hour. I've run out of work to do, and the sun outside is beckoning. I wish there was a bench in front of my hut where I could sit and enjoy the sunshine, but no, we're not allowed to do things like that. It's a waste of time. If we want time for contemplation, we pray to the Angel, not sit around lazily. Even when it's as sunny as it is now.

It's getting warm inside, so I open the window, letting in some muggy air. It's heavy with moisture, ready to turn into rain later this evening, or maybe during the night. It's been pretty dry recently, especially for Scottish summers, so the gardeners will be thankful for some rain. We grow most of our food ourselves - well, other people do. It's not fitting for the Prophet's wife to crawl on the ground picking weeds. The only times I'm kneeling on the floor is when Andros tells me to.

My smile disappears at that thought. As much as I feel

guilty that I'm not currently taking the community's sins upon me, I don't miss the punishments, the pain.

No. It's selfish, I shouldn't be thinking that. It's an honour to have that role. The Angel will reward me. Soon, we'll ascend and everything will be alright.

I lean against the window frame, not quite ready to leave my position in the heat of the sun. I run my hands over the warm, rough wood. Andros built this hut for me, together with some of the other men. They've built the entire village from scratch. It's rustic and simple, but it works. It's my little home, my refuge.

My fingers reach something soft, not wood. It's a piece of paper, folded several times and folded so it fits in the tiny gap where the window sill meets the wall. Another secret message? I hesitate before opening it. My breathing is getting quicker. This is forbidden. This can't be good. I should throw the note away or wait for Andros and have him read it. There shouldn't be secrets in this community. That's against the Angel's wishes. Once a week, we confess our secrets and doubts to our confession partners. Mine is Andros, of course, but the rest of the community are usually paired up with people of a similar age. If someone has done something particularly bad, the listener will report it to the Prophet, but most of the times, the sinful thoughts aren't big enough for it to come to that. We're good people, all living with one sole aim: to reach ascension and be with the Angel.

With shaking fingers, I unfold the note. I can't help it. I need to know. Maybe it's just a joke.

Don't do it. Life is precious.

What? I was expecting yet another reassuring message,

something about holding on or staying put until help comes, like the ones before. But not this. Don't do what?

I read it again and again until my shaking gets less. Life is precious. Of course it is, I never said it wasn't. Why do they feel they need to tell me?

I crumple the note in my fist and slam the window shut, almost hoping that whoever left the message there can see my reaction. I want to throw the paper away, but instead, I stuff it into my little hiding place together with the other ones. If anyone ever finds them... well, let's not think about that.

I flinch when someone knocks at the door and quickly shove the mattress back to its old position, covering my sins and secrets. I grab my crown from a hook on the wall and put it on; Andros doesn't like it when people see me without it. It's a constant reminder that I'm his, and the Angel's. Their property, their tool.

"Yes?" I call, making sure my robe is sitting correctly.

"It's Martin, the doctor. I need your help!" He sounds frantic and I run to the door, opening it wide. His cheeks are red and there's a sheen of sweat on his forehead. He's panting as if he's run here. "One of the women is giving birth, but they're not letting me inside." He's talking almost too quickly to understand. "Please, you need to tell them that I can help. The baby is premature and it might not be able to survive without medical intervention."

Daisy. She's the only one pregnant at the moment, and I'm pretty sure it's Andros's child. She's not due for at least six weeks though. It's hard to tell without ultrasound and those kind of things, but she's definitely not big enough to be giving birth yet.

"Is she in her house?" I ask and step outside, turning left as soon as he nods. I walk fast, but Martin quickly overtakes me, so I break into a run, hurrying towards Daisy's home. It's almost at the other end of the compound, so when we reach it, I'm just as out of breath as the doctor. The screams tear at my heart, and a quick look at Martin proves that he's feeling the same. A mother in pain. The fate of her child unknown.

I take a deep breath and push against the door - but it doesn't budge. It's locked. We never lock our doors, most of them don't even have locks.

"Daisy!" I shout. "Let me in!"

"Is he with you?" Rose calls from inside. Good, at least there are other women with her.

"The doctor? Yes."

"He can't come inside. No men allowed, the Angel wouldn't like it. He might punish the baby for it."

"The baby might die if you don't let me in!" Martin shouts in exasperation. He looks as if he's about to kick the door in, his usual composure gone.

"Go away!" Rose yells, desperation and determination mingling in her voice. "I will not let your ignorance harm the baby."

"My ignorance?" the doctor splutters. "Have you ever thought that the Angel may have sent me here to help? That he wants me to save the mother and baby?" He turns to me. "Tell her to let me in. You're his wife."

I freeze. He wants me to intervene. He believes I have some kind of authority. Well, I don't. Andros may have decided to call me the Princess, but I have no powers. On the contrary, that title sets me apart from the other women, stops me from being one of them. They don't care about me, and they certainly won't listen to me.

Daisy screams again, a wail full of fear and pain. I take a deep breath and slam my fist against the door. She needs help.

"Let us in!"

"No!" Rose shouts at the same time as another woman calls, "It's coming!"

It's Myrtle, one of the oldest women in the community. She's a grandmother, although she's never told us about her family. Once you become part of the Angel's family, you leave your mortal family behind.

Martin stands next to me and pushes against the door, trying to break in. It doesn't budge. Daisy's husband is a carpenter and right now, I wish he wasn't so talented. This is probably the sturdiest door in the entire village.

More screams from inside. "It's in the wrong position," Myrtle says loud enough for us to hear it. "She's bleeding too much."

Angel, help us.

"She might die if I don't help her," Martin yells, hammering against the door, his fists clenched with anger. "How can you let that happen?"

Something is pushed against the door from the inside. "Go away, you're angering the Angel!"

The sound of our hands on wood changes, becomes deeper. Rose must have blocked the door. Why is she doing this instead of helping Daisy? Is she really that worried that a man might see Daisy in this position, or is there another reason?

Suddenly, the cries stop and Daisy falls silent. I stop

knocking and put my ear against the door, almost hoping that she'll start to screams begin again, or that the cry of a baby breaks the silence. Nothing. All I can hear is hurried footsteps inside, and a low, inaudible whisper.

"What's going on?" I shout, my worry reflecting in Martin's expression.

Nobody replies. My fingernails rake over the smooth wood of the door, the tension in me threatening to turn into tears. Please, Angel, let them be alive. Let the baby live, it's innocent, it's not done anything wrong. Don't take them.

My prayer is useless. It's too late.

When the two women inside begin to chant the Angel's mantra, I let myself sink to the ground, my back against the door that stopped us from saving two lives.

"Suffering brings peace.
Pain is salvation.
The Angel is our shield and our refuge."

Ten

We don't do funerals. We don't mourn. We hope that the Angel has taken them into his realm, and if not, then there's nothing we can do.

Life goes on. Andros returns. The wounds that had healed break open again as he starts to work on his canvas again. He keeps me in my house, only letting me leave for prayers.

Nothing has changed, and yet, inside of me, there's turmoil. I don't know what to think anymore. What to do. What to say. What to confess. Tomorrow is the day of confession, and I need to decide how much to tell Andros.

That in itself is a sin. It's wrong. I should tell him everything, like before. Like I used to. I need to tell him that I have doubts, that I think Daisy could have been saved. That her baby might still be alive. That things done in the Angel's name don't automatically have to be good.

But that's blasphemy, isn't it? The Angel guides us, helps us be better people. Maybe he wanted Rose and

Myrtle to prevent the doctor from helping. Maybe he had plans for Daisy and the baby. Maybe they're now by his side, forever in Paradise.

But what if he didn't?

I'm glad I don't have to be amongst the others right now. It gives me time to think without having to hide my feelings. I worry that they can see the doubt in my eyes. Andros can, I'm sure of it. He knows so much, far more than he should. Sometimes he looks at me and it feels like he can see the inside of my soul. Maybe the Angel looks through his eyes.

I didn't even know Daisy that well. She was only twenty and came here with her husband, who'd been a follower of the Angel for some time. They seemed happy together, and even though the child likely wasn't his, I'm sure they would have been a good family.

Now, he's a widower who isn't supposed to grieve. He hides his sadness well, but it shows in the sag of his shoulders, the crinkles of his shirt, the way he chants the mantras even louder than before. I want to go to him and tell him how sorry I am, but that's not right on so many levels.

Instead, I stay as I am, playing my role as the Prophet's wife, while inside the doubt is eating away at my faith in the Angel.

No, maybe not the Angel. I still believe in him, I trust him. Who I doubt is Andros and the rules of this community.

He's asked me to come and see him in his office. It's strange, usually he just turns up at my door, no warning at all, but this time, he's sent Rose to give me his message. She looks at me curiously as I read his note, but doesn't say anything.

"I'll just need to get changed," I tell her, and she nods and walks away, leaving me in peace. I don't actually need to change, but I want a moment to think. What does Andros want from me? It's probably something public, something where other people are involved. I hope it's not another public punishment. Those are the worst.

I sigh and put my golden crown on my head, grimacing as I do so. I hate that thing, and yet, it's my burden to wear.

Not many people are out and about; it's just before lunch time when everyone is busy. I hurry over the square to the community building in which Andros has his office. He doesn't spend a lot of time in there, so I've only been in to visit him a couple of times.

I knock on the door and he calls for me to enter. The office is dark, for some reason he's pulled the curtains shut. It's so nice and sunny outside, but I know better than to ask why he's spending time in a dark room.

"We'll ascend on Friday," he says by way of greeting. "It's the anniversary of my first vision, so I think it's fitting that it's the day we finally travel to the Angel."

I stare at him. Despite him talking about Ascension more and more during the past couple of weeks, it comes as a shock. This week. Friday. Ascension.

"You don't look happy," he observes, and I quickly put a smile on my lips.

"I'm just surprised. I thought we'd need more time to be ready."

He points at several boxes stacked up in the corner behind him. "I've got all the supplies, enough for everyone in the community. You and I will help the others reach the Angel, and then we'll ascend together, as husband and wife." He smiles widely. "I can't wait to finally show you his magnificence. The Angel is overwhelming in my visions and dreams, and in reality he will be even more radiant. We will sit by his side, the others at our feet, and we'll be happy for all eternity." He walks around his desk until he stands in front of me and lifts my chin with a tap of his finger. "We'll be together forever, sweet little bird. Nobody will ever get between us."

I suppress a shudder. I want to ascend, of course I do, but I don't want to spend the rest of my life – no, not life, eternity - with Andros. I don't think his cruelty will vanish once we've ascended. Unless the Angel intervenes, it will stay how it is now, the beatings, the pain. Will he still be able to use me as his canvas, or do wounds heal immediately in Paradise? I'm not brave enough to ask.

He leans down and kisses me hard, his lips tight against mine. I know better than to struggle. For the first time, I realise that this will be my fate forever. There is no escape from Andros.

Unless... I part my lips in surprise at the direction my thoughts are taking, but my husband takes it as an excuse to plunge his tongue into my mouth. This time, I can't help shivering in disgust, but luckily, he interprets it as arousal and groans.

"We'll be together forever," he whispers when he finally breaks the kiss and lets me step back. "You'll always be mine."

Eleven

For now, Andros has told me to keep the impending ascension quiet. He's busy preparing, although I'm not quite sure what that involves. I think I'm the only one who knows that it's almost time.

It's Tuesday today, only three more days. He's going to have to make arrangements for the children soon. The plan was to have one couple stay behind to look after them, but Andros hasn't announced who that's going to be yet. They're going to be disappointed to be prevented to ascend with the rest of us, but someone needs to prepare the next generation of believers. We can't be the last. The Angel relies on us to get more followers for him. Maybe he'll create a new Prophet, who knows.

There's a noise from outside my house and I jump up, expecting Andros, but the door stays shut. Instead, a piece of paper has been pushed underneath the door. Another message. They've become less frequent, although I still get regular food gifts through the window. Fruit, mostly, but yesterday it was a bar of chocolate. I'm feeling less and less guilty about eating them.

I snatch up the envelope and rip it open. The paper inside only has a single word scribbled on it.

WHEN?

I stuff it in my pocket and open the door, but of course, there's nobody to be seen. Some villagers are walking around in the distance, but none of them even look in the direction of my house. The mysterious messenger is very adept at staying hidden. Now, he wants me to answer for the first time.

I close the door and lean against it, looking at the message once again. When. He must mean the ascension. Nothing else makes sense. There's a tiny pencil in the envelope, only as long as my little finger. I should be questioning whether to answer, whether to finally hand the notes to Andros, but instead, I write FRIDAY on the back of the paper.

Usually, my secret deliveries come through my window – which is why I always leave it open now, unless it's raining – so I fold the message as small as I can and squeeze it in the gap between the glass and the frame. Hopefully, he'll find it there.

Strange though. How does he know that the ascension is close? Maybe he didn't mean that after all? Maybe he wanted to meet? Or... why am I even thinking that it's a he?

My head is spinning; I need air. I put on my crown and make sure my clothes are covering me in all the important places, before stepping outside, taking a deep breath.

The smell of fresh bread tickles my nose. Strange, the kitchen is quite far away from my house, but it seems the wind is strong enough today to carry the scent all the way to me. I smile and head towards the promise of food.

The only person in the community kitchen is one of the novices. His red robe is covered in flour and he's rolled up his sleeves, exposing ample muscle as he kneads a giant ball of dough.

I've only seen him from afar, during prayers, but haven't actually spoken to him. Now that he's not wearing his hood, I can finally look at him a little closer. His hair is cut short like it's the custom, with the ends a tiny bit redder than the roots. Maybe he had his hair dyed before he came here?

His back is broad and muscular, stretching the robe. I remember seeing him for the very first time and thinking that the other two recruits would have less of a problem with the small amounts of food we're allowed, but now that I know he's working in the kitchen, I feel less bad for him.

"Can I help you?" he asks without looking up.

"It smells nice," I splutter, not quite sure what to say – I'm not supposed to be here. He's a man, I'm a woman, and we're alone. That's as forbidden as it gets. "I should go," I add and turn around.

"Wait," he calls before I can leave. "Can you help me with something? The other cook is ill today, and I don't think I'm going to get everything ready by lunch time."

I hesitate. I really shouldn't be here. I should leave and find a man who can help him instead of me.

"Please?" he asks again. He's turned around and is

watching me curiously. His face is just as covered in flour as his robe, and his hands are sticky with bread dough.

"Okay then." I close the door behind me. "What shall I do?"

He raises an eyebrow as if he's surprised that I stayed, but then he turns around and tears his big ball of dough into two parts. "Could you knead this? The bread will be better if it's worked thoroughly, but I don't have the time."

I nod and roll up my sleeves before noticing that it's not proper. Too late. And anyway, this is for the good of the community. People will be unhappy if there's no lunch.

I start to knead the dough, enjoying the strange blend of stickiness and smoothness. The soothing smell of yeast fills the room, mixing with another. "Soup?" I ask and the man nods.

"Pea soup. It's pretty much ready, so all we need to get done now is the bread. I should have probably made the bread first, but I'm still new to this."

I'm tempted to ask him what he did before he came here, but we don't do that. Our old lives don't matter now that we've found the Angel to guide us.

We knead the bread in silence. It's a peaceful task, despite my arms slowly beginning to ache from the unfamiliar strain. I'm not used to manual labour. One of my sleeves falls down and I roll it back up again, higher this time to make sure it stays in place.

I go back to working the dough, but stop when I feel the man's eyes on me. He's staring at my upper arm, his expression darkening. I look down at myself and cringe. By rolling up my sleeve I've exposed the bruises covering my skin. Andros always makes sure they stay in areas usually hidden beneath my clothes, but now I've made a mistake.

I look at the table and tug at the sleeve until it falls to my elbow again. The relaxed silence between us has turned uncomfortable and I'm tempted to leave. Everybody knows how Andros treats me, but most people haven't seen the evidence of it. Least of all the novices.

I wait for him to say something, but he stays quiet and we fall back into our rhythm of kneading the bread, turning it, stretching it.

"I'm Noran," he says finally, surprising me.

"Laya," I answer.

"I know."

Silence again.

He clears his throat. "How long have you been here?"

"Since the beginning." I smile at the memory of how we found this place, how we bought the land, how Andros and I planned the layout of the village. We were so full of hope and enthusiasm back then. Everything was new.

"Of course, you're his wife." He nods, more to himself than to me. "Did you marry before you came here or after?"

"After," I answer before I realise that we shouldn't be having this conversation. It's too personal. "Are you liking it here?"

He doesn't comment on my change of topic. "It's very peaceful. It's different than I expected though."

"Different how?"

"People are so... normal. I was expecting – please don't take this in the wrong way – hippies and alternative folks, not people of all ages and backgrounds who wouldn't stand out at all in a normal crowd."

I shrug. "The Angel's call can reach anyone, no matter who they are. That's the beauty of it."

"True, otherwise I wouldn't be here," he says, putting his dough to one side and pulling a stack of baking trays from a shelf beneath the table. "Can you make six equal balls?"

I nod and get on with my task, meticulously separating my big ball into six smaller parts. I'm a bit of a perfectionist sometimes. Noran takes them and forms them into loaves before placing them on the trays and using a knife to cut a pattern onto the top. "Makes the crust nicer," he explains.

Without warning, the door opens and Connor steps in. When he sees me, he stops in his tracks and looks at me wide-eyed. I must be covered in flour, just like Noran, and my sleeves are still rolled up.

"What are you doing here?" he asks, confusion and a trace of anger colouring his voice.

"I was helping," I stutter, before quickly patting off my clothes and heading towards the door. "I should go."

"Yes, you should," Connor mutters and I almost run out before he can say any more.

I shouldn't have done this. I shouldn't have been there. I should never have stayed. But inside of me, a spark of happiness is dancing wildly and I can't suppress the smile curving my lips. I hurry home before someone can see it.

$\mathcal{T}$welve

Andros doesn't mention the bread incident when he visits me at night, so maybe Connor didn't tell him. His whipping isn't more forceful than usual, but that doesn't mean it stops me from screaming in pain.

"Do you think this will feel just as good when we're in Paradise, little dove?" he asks when he has finished and kneels by my side, softly running his hands over the wounds he's inflicted. I don't reply. It doesn't feel good, not to me. And if it does to him... it's only more proof of how depraved he is. I get that I need to be punished, but he shouldn't be enjoying it.

He doesn't seem bothered by my silence.

"I think it will be magnificent. Maybe the Angel will watch. Maybe he'll even take part. Wouldn't you like that, sweet girl? Being taken by the Angel, that would be the highest honour imaginable. Maybe he'd even give you a child. You'd be like Mary."

I whimper at the thought. In my mind, the Angel is

benevolent, gentle, kind, not at all like the Angel Andros is describing right now.

"Do you really think he'd do that?" I whisper, my voice hoarse from screaming.

"I do," Andros says enthusiastically. "He's been showing me more and more visions of how I'm punishing you, so I believe he'll want to watch once we're in Paradise for real. Maybe we should bring forward ascension. Everything is ready, there's no point in waiting. Yes, let's do it tomorrow. The sooner we ascend, the quicker I can watch the Angel take you."

He keeps running his hands over my burning back, increasing the agony of the bloody streaks he's painted on my skin.

I thought the pain would end once we've ascended. Now, it seems like it'll never be over. I'm always going to be the Prophet's canvas, always in pain, always suffering.

"We'll do it tomorrow," Andros whispers as he lies down beside me and squeezes a hand between my legs. "Tomorrow we will leave this Earth and become immortal."

I didn't sleep, of course I didn't. Andros left in the early hours of the morning to prepare everything, telling me to pray and ready myself.

By the time the sun starts to rise, my ankle is hurting painfully. I've been thinking about running away too much. All this time I've been working towards ascension, but now, I am scared of it. Not because of the process of ascending, but of what awaits me once we've stepped into Paradise. I imagined a peaceful, happy existence under the loving guidance of the Angel. Now, everything has changed. That image has been twisted and turned into a nightmare that I won't be able to escape from. Paradise is final, there's nowhere to move on from there.

Someone knocks on the door and I expect Rose, there to clean my wounds.

"Come in!" I rasp, but nobody enters. I wait for a minute, but curiosity is stronger than my pain and I stumble to the door. I don't care that I'm naked. Right now, I don't care about anything.

A small plate waits for me on my doorstep, a sandwich on top, made from two thick slices of the bread I baked yesterday. I quickly take it inside, hunger spreading in my belly.

I know it's probably not just food though, and when I pull the bread slices apart, my suspicion is confirmed. There's a note hidden inside, wrapped in clingfilm.

WE KNOW. HELP IS COMING. DON'T TAKE IT.

It's no longer just one messenger. We. More than one. Don't take the help? Or don't take the poison that Andros is preparing? Probably the latter, it doesn't make sense otherwise.

I hide the message in the usual spot and start to nibble on the sandwich, but I don't even notice the taste. Help is coming. Do I want help? Do I need it?

For once, I know the answer.

Yes, I do. I want to get away. I no longer want to stay here, and I certainly don't want to ascend to an eternity of pain and humiliation.

My ankle begins to throb again, but I ignore it.

I'm getting out of here, no matter the cost.

I was expecting this day to be different from our usual routine, but when I go outside, nothing seems to have changed. People are going about their daily business, one of the babies is screaming somewhere to my right, and the sun is shining, warming the ground beneath my naked feet.

It's a day like any other. Nobody knows yet that it's going to be their last day on Earth, unless someone intervenes. I'm not sure I want them to stop the ascension for everyone. It wouldn't be fair. Just because I no longer want to do it, doesn't mean that the rest of the believers shouldn't get the chance.

"What are you doing here?" Andros is suddenly in front of me, his arms crossed over his chest, his eyes flaring with anger. "You shouldn't be outside."

"I wanted to see if they need help in the office," I mutter, automatically bowing my head and taking on a demure position. He's trained me well.

"They don't. Go back home and stay there until midday prayer when I announce the ascension. I don't want anybody else to know yet."

I nod and head back to my house, but not before I can hear him whisper, "I'm going to punish you for this later." I'm not sure if he means before or after the ascension.

At home, I sit on the floor, staring at the statue of the Angel. I have nothing to do, not even books to copy.

Nothing to read, either. All I have are my swirling thoughts in my head and the Angel looking down on me.

I stare back at him defiantly.

"You won't have me," I tell him. "Not if you're like Andros."

I search his features for any sign of the benevolence I saw in them in the past, but all I see is stern lines and hard eyes. I could easily imagine him raising my husband's whip. No, I won't let him. I won't be their victim any longer.

I get up and turn the statue around until he looks at the wall. I don't want him to watch me. Something catches my eye on its pedestal and I take a closer look. There's something small and black wedged into a crack in the wood, just below the Angel's flowing gown. I pick at it with my fingernails until I manage to pull it out. It's a tiny microphone with a short antenna, no bigger than my finger nail. A bug. My house is being bugged. No wonder they knew that the ascension has been pulled forward.

I should be angry, but it's actually a relief to know that someone has been listening in. They'll know what Andros has been doing. There are witnesses. Even if they will never tell anybody, it feels good to know that I'm not alone. Someone cares.

I smile and push the bug back in its old position, before turning the Angel statue around again. I hate him seeing me, but I don't want anyone else to find the microphone. It's my little secret.

Now I'm back to not knowing what to do. I look around the room. It's been my house for years, but it's never quite felt like home. There are no pictures on the walls, no decoration at all. My white robes are hanging from hooks on the wall, and my simple white and beige clothes are folded neatly on a shelf that was once a shoe rack. That, a mattress on the floor and a small sink in a corner is the extent of my furniture. Even prisoners have more. I smile grimly. I've never thought that before. I'm changing, my thoughts are getting more rebellious. I should be scared of that, I should be repenting, confessing to Andros, praying to the Angel, but all I do is sit there, smiling and waiting for what's going to happen next.

Thirteen

The Prophet doesn't mention ascension until the end of the midday prayer. Only when everyone is ready to leave, does he lift his voice again, surprising everyone.

"We will be ascending tonight," he announces. Gasps and shouts are all around me, and it takes a moment for Andros to get their attention again. "The Angel has told me to do it this evening, which is sooner than expected, but he in his infinite wisdom has decreed that we shall join him on this very day. Everything is prepared, so now it's time for all of us to meditate and pray that the Angel will let us sit by his side. I have written a letter to the authorities to explain that we have ascended in good faith. I have also sent the words of the Angel to supporters and libraries across the world, so that other people may find the true path and follow us, the very first believers." He smiles and opens his arms wide. "Are there any questions?"

I think most of them are dumbstruck and surprised,

but one woman, Jasmine, steps forward. "What about the children?"

Andros's smile widens. "They will ascend with us. They will grow up in Paradise, guided by the Angel's wisdom and grace."

I swallow hard. That had never been the plan before. The babies were supposed to stay behind, not ascend. Jasmine nods and steps back into the line of women, but her expression has hardened into an unreadable mask. I wonder if it's fear or determination that she's trying to hide.

"Will it hurt?" one of the men asks, but I can't see who it is.

"I'm told it's painless," Andros explains. "But even if it does, it will be a small price to pay."

"I'm not asking for myself, Prophet," the man continues after a moment of silence. "But my wife is very sensitive to pain, and I'm worried she might suffer."

"Suffering is peace," Andros recites warmly. "But if it reassures you, I will have my own wife ascend first to show you all the way."

It's like he's kicked me in the chest. Me, first. No, it can't be. He said we'd ascend together, the last ones, and I was hoping that help might arrive in time that everybody else can ascend and then help me escape. I want them all to reach the Angel, I really do. They deserve to be in his light.

Other questions are being asked, but my ears are buzzing and I'm fighting the bile rising up in my throat. I want to be sick, I want to run, but all I can do is stand there and wait for the inevitable end.

. . .

We're told to wash ourselves and put on new clothes. I do it in a haze, going through the motions like I'm not really there. I shower, shave my scalp one last time, slip into my cleanest robe. I don't worry that my wounds will stain the cloth. I will never have to wash it again.

When we're all washed and cleansed, we assemble in the community hall for prayer.

Discipline leads to redemption.

Suffering brings peace.

Obedience inspires happiness.

Pain is salvation.

The Angel is our shield and our refuge.

We repeat the mantra over and over, my lips forming the words automatically. Then Andros stands, preaches about what awaits us on the other side, repeating the visions he's told us about over and over, before we're back to mantras. In a way, they give me comfort. They're familiar, soothing.

We kneel for hours until the light shining through the high windows begins to turn a light shade of red.

Andros stands and the mantra ends, the echo of our voices still reverberating through the room.

"Novices, you will have to decide now whether you are ready or whether you want to stay on Earth for a while longer, before ascending on your own. I believe you have learned enough to successfully ascend, but I'm leaving the decision to you."

The three men in their red robes stand in the front row and I watch as they turn to each other as if they're taking the decision together.

"We will ascend." It's Martin who replies, the doctor. His voice is clear and determined, so unlike the way I feel.

Andros smiles. "Good. I'm proud of you." He turns to me and holds out a hand. "Princess, it's time."

I stay where I am, frozen, unable to move. This can't be happening. It's too soon. I'm not ready, I never will be.

"Laya," he says, his smile still there but his eyes have grown hard. "Come here."

I know what's expected of me. I need to be a role model, unafraid, strong, determined, the perfect servant of the Angel. Maybe it won't be so bad. Maybe the Angel will be as good as I imagined him.

I force my shaking body to move to Andros's side. He puts an arm around my shoulders, pressing me close to him, more shackles than embrace.

"Be strong," he whispers, before turning to the other side where Connor has appeared with a crate of bottles. Andros takes one of them and holds it up so all can see. "This is our way of ascension. Drink at least half a bottle, then lie down and pray. It won't take long. If you need help, let me know. I will be the last to go so I can make sure you have all ascended safely."

He removes his arm from my shoulders to open the bottle. Now would be my chance to run, but I can't move. My legs are shaking so much that I'm threatening to fall, but then Andros's arm is around my waist again, steadying me.

"Pray with me as my wife ascends," he hollers and puts the bottle to my lips, tilting it until the liquid kisses my lips. I don't open them and the poison pools around my mouth.

"Drink," Andros hisses so only I can hear. I just look at

him in defiance. I'm not going to. He frowns and suddenly pinches my side so hard that I gasp and open my mouth – and drink the liquid he's now pouring down my throat. It tastes like apple juice, fruity and sweet, not at all like something that's about to rip me from my mortal body. I swallow as more and more of it fills my mouth, drinking the poison while watching a smile spread across Andros's face.

My vision is going blurry much quicker than I expected, and my legs finally give in. Andros gently lowers me to the ground, his lips brushing against mine. "See you soon, little dove. Wait for me."

His hand cups my cheek, but then it's gone and he's no longer there. Everything is spinning, I can't see, the sounds are disappearing, but I can still feel a sharp pinch in my arm and hear the loud bangs that are like drums welcoming me to Paradise.

DISCIPLINE LEADS TO REDEMPTION.

SUFFERING BRINGS PEACE.

OBEDIENCE INSPIRES HAPPINESS.

PAIN IS SALVATION.

THE ANGEL IS OUR SHIELD AND OUR REFUGE.

Part Two

Fourteen

The Angel never comes to take me home. Instead, the tubes and beeps keep me alive, just about, edging on the far rim of life.

At first, I'm not aware, but slowly, I notice more and more of what's happening around me, even if I can't move or reply. I'm in a strange twilight land, not quite awake, not quite asleep.

They're talking about me. First, wondering whether I'll make it. Then, asking how long it'll be until I wake. They want to ask me questions, so many questions, but all I want is sleep. In sleep, I'm happy, alive and far, far away from all that's happened. My dreams are set in the times before I met Andros, showing me memories I'd thought I'd buried deep away. My parents, my family.

The day they take the tube out of my throat is when I almost wake up, but I'm not quite ready yet. I don't think I'll ever be.

When my eyes open for the first time, I close them again. They know I'm awake, they talk to me, they try and make me eat. I refuse it all. I don't know what I want to happen. Do I want to ascend, leave it all behind? Fulfil the destiny I've been working towards all these years? Or do I want to live in a world without the Angel, without the Prophet and his guidance?

I can't give it up. It's entwined within my very essence, my soul. I believe in the Angel and I always will. Maybe, one day, when I'm brave enough, I will ascend, but not now. Not when Andros is there, too. Maybe if I learn to be stronger here on Earth, I will be able to defy him in Paradise. Yes. Let that be my mission.

I wake to the sound of a familiar voice, but it takes me a while to place it. Martin.

"Are you awake?" he asks and I open my eyes, taking in my surroundings for the first time. I already know I'm in hospital, so I'm not surprised by the plain white walls and ceiling. The blinds are drawn shut, letting only dim streaks of light into the room.

"See, I told you she needed someone familiar to visit her," Martin says to someone in the background, "and now you can leave us."

The door is shut and a chair pulled close. Then he's in my field of vision and I can look at the doctor, the novice, the stranger who cared for me when Andros had whipped me bloody. It's strange to see him in normal clothes and not the crimson robes he used to wear.

"How are you feeling?" he asks gently, his eyes flickering to the beeping monitors above me.

I have no idea how I'm feeling, so I stay quiet, just

watching him. A beard is beginning to grow on his chin, already more than just a shadow. It must have been several days since he last shaved, which means that the day of ascension is at least as long ago.

"What happened?" I ask, but my throat is so dry that I don't get the words out properly. Martin picks up a glass with a straw from the little bedside table on my right and holds it to my lips. I drink greedily, only now noticing how thirsty I am. My lips feel chafed and raw against the plastic straw.

When he takes the glass away, I swallow and ask the same question again. This time, it's more or less audible.

He sits back down and looks at me, his expression darkening. "We almost lost you. When Andros decided that you'd be first to take the poison, he surprised us. We were already scrambling to get everything ready because we'd been assuming that he'd do the ceremony on Friday. Luckily, we heard him telling you, so we managed to get reinforcements in just in time. When you drank the poison, they stormed the hall. I had a variety of antidotes with me, and I gave you an injection immediately, but Andros's mixture was stronger than we could have anticipated. We pumped out your stomach and treated you on scene as well as we could, but it was damn close. Luckily we had a helicopter to bring you to hospital straight away."

His eyes flicker back to the monitors.

"How bad?" I ask, not quite sure if I'm able to form longer sentences yet. It hurts when I speak.

"A few more days and the drugs should be out of your system. Once you get out of hospital, you'll be weak for another few days, maybe a week, then everything should be back to normal." He grimaces. "Well, as normal as it can be. Everything will change for you, but we'll try our best to make it as easy for you as possible."

"We?"

"Ah. Yes. Andros has been taken into custody, and all of the other villagers are held in safe places, under observation. Some have tried to take their own lives since we rescued them, so they're all on suicide watch." He runs a hand through his hair and sighs. "We'd heard rumours of abuse and human rights violations in the cult, but we didn't expect a mass suicide attempt."

I stare at him. What is he saying? Why is he using those words?

He was part of us, he was learning to be one of us. Now he talks as if we were all crazy, as if he's so different from us. I want to turn away from him, but my body isn't complying, so I close my eyes instead.

"Laya? Shit, sorry, Leek is the one trained to do this, I'm just doing this because you know me best out of the three of us. I should probably shut up now."

I don't reply. Mass suicide. No, that's wrong. Ascension isn't death. It's so much more than that.

"There's going to be a trial. I don't know yet how many people will be involved, but for now, Andros is the main defendant. They want you to be a witness, Laya. The key witness. But we know that Andros has people outside the actual village, and he's made threats against anyone who will testify against him. Which means that you'll be in witness protection from now on until the trial."

I open my eyes again to stare at him. "I can't."

He's my husband. The Prophet. I can't be the reason

for him to go to prison. That would be so wrong. I should be at his side, not testifying against him. No.

"I know everything's strange and overwhelming for you just now," Martin says soothingly. "You don't need to do anything while you're still here. We'll be taking your statement once you're better, and we'll make sure you're safe."

He keeps saying that, so I ask him again. "We?"

"My two colleagues and I. You know us as Martin, Noran and Owen, but we have other names, and we weren't really recruits. We're police, Laya, and we're going to make sure Andros is punished for what he did to you."

Fifteen

People keep checking on me, but I don't react to them. Martin said he'd come again, but so far, he's not returned. It's been two days, I think. I'm feeling much stronger, and I've been able to eat by myself again, removing the need for the feeding tube. Thank the Angel for that. There's still a cannula in my arm, but that's a lot less uncomfortable than a tube stuck in your nose.

There's a TV in the room, but I don't want to switch it on. I've lived without one for so long, I'm scared to find out about the state of the world. I've not watched or read the news for years. I have no idea what's going on out there. I couldn't tell you who our prime minister is, or if there are any wars happening in the world right now. There probably are, though. Sometimes, Andros would preach about what he'd seen on his trips away from the community: pollution, poverty, child neglect, crime. Hearing about those things always make me glad to live in such a peaceful place.

I know that eventually, I'll have to face the world, but for now, I enjoy the solitude while it lasts. Most of the nurses have given up trying to start a conversation with me, and I don't blame them. I don't reply, I stare at the ceiling, I'm as passive as it gets. I can't bring myself to react to the people around me. Everything is so different, so strange. Maybe, if I stay in stasis, life will stay as it was. Maybe everything will go back to normal.

What I miss most isn't Andros and the other people of the community. No, it's the Angel. I felt so close to him in the village, surrounded by statues of him and the daily prayers. Here, I feel like I'm far away from him, like he's no longer with me wherever I go. The comfortable knowledge that he's watching out for me is flaking at the edges. I'm lonely without his presence. I wish there was a statue of him here in the room. Maybe I can get one wherever I will go from here.

Martin has said that I'll be in witness protection, even though I have told him that I won't go to court. He said that as long as there was a tiny chance of me testifying, he'd be able to get me into the programme. Somewhere safe, a new home. I can refuse to speak at the trial even on the day it takes place, he's promised that. That's why I agreed to sign the form. I have no intention of testifying, but if this gives me somewhere to live in peace, then I'll take it, no matter how selfish that seems. I have no one left, nowhere to turn. I broke all ties with my family when I joined the Angel's followers. My friends and my husband are being held by the police. I'm all on my own.

A knock on the door distracts me from my morbid thoughts. An unexpected man comes into the room and immediately sits on the chair by my bed. Owen. What is he doing here?

He looks at me with his crystal blue eyes, then smiles. "Hello."

I lift an eyebrow at him, but don't say anything. He's the one who came to me to ask about ascension. He seemed very interested back then, but now that I know that he's with the police, it makes sense. He was a little too curious for a new novice.

"Andy wanted to come himself, but he's been called away on family matters, so I thought I'd come and visit you."

"Andy?" What is he talking about?

"Oh, of course. You don't know our names. Sorry, this is a bit strange, introducing myself even though I've known you for weeks. I'm Quentin. Andrew is who you know as Martin, and Noran is Leek."

Martin, Noran, Owen. Now they're Andrew, Leek, Quentin. Their names are no longer in consecutive alphabetical order. Somehow, that annoys me.

"Leek?" I ask. "Like the vegetable?"

Owen... no, Quentin smiles. "His parents were hippies who didn't believe in normal names. His brother is called Sunset, I kid you not."

I don't return his smile. Different names. Different lives. It was all a lie. I thought I could like them. Maybe get to know them, once we'd ascended and the gender separation rules had been relaxed a little like Andros had promised. I was looking forward to maybe becoming their friend.

I swallow hard and ask the question that's burning on my tongue. "Was any of it real?"

He doesn't reply immediately, which tells me all I need to know.

"Please leave," I tell him, turning to my side, facing away from him.

He doesn't move. I wish he'd go. I prefer to be alone with my thoughts and the silence of this room.

"I really was interested," he says quietly. "I found the concept of your belief system fascinating. I've always been interested in religions and wrote my thesis on the Jonestown cult. So when they offered me the chance to investigate a new and different religion, I took it. So in that way, my interest was genuine."

"But you don't believe in the Angel," I whisper, drawing the blanket further around me. The thought of their betrayal is making me shiver.

"No, I don't. I'm sorry, but I don't think I believe in anything. What fascinates me is what other people believe in, and how that drives their actions."

"So we were like research subjects for you?" My voice has turned bitter, but I think I have reason for that.

"No," he says emphatically, his eyes sparkling. "You're people, and I wanted to help you. Especially when you ran into me that very first time and I saw what he was doing to you. I wish I could have taken you away right then, but we needed to stay until the ascension ceremony. We needed him to take action before we could intervene."

"Why did you even care? The police, I mean? It's our life, and ascension is our decision."

"I think if more than sixty people suddenly take their own lives, that is of interest to everyone. It needs to be investigated, and prevented, of course. There were children involved, Laya, and I saw from your expression when Andros announced it, that you didn't agree with that either."

"No," I mutter. "Not the children."

"See? And just like you feel about the children, I feel about all of you. The entire community. It's always wrong to take a life, whether it's your own or someone else's. I'm sorry it all ended how it did, but it's better this way." He sighs. "I've seen the pictures. When you were first admitted, they had to collect forensic evidence and take photographs of your injuries. How long did he treat you like that? A year? Longer? Some of the scars looked old."

I don't reply. I don't need to, he can listen to the explanations from the doctors. That's all he's interested in anyway. He wouldn't understand how punishing me was important to Andros. How it took away the sins of the entire community.

It's good though to be in less pain than I usually am. They've put dressings on the wounds. One of the nurses said that some of them would have needed stitches, but that it was too long ago since they were inflicted. They've given me painkillers as well, the first time I've taken medicine like that in ages. Andros was always against manmade medicine, but right now, I'm grateful for it. My ankle doesn't hurt anymore, either.

"Your ankle?" Quentin asks and I realise that I must have spoken aloud. "The metal band? I thought that was an old injury?"

I turn onto my back again. Now that we're talking, I don't really want him to go after all. Maybe conversation is better than silence.

"It hurt sometimes," I admit, "when I was thinking of... stuff." I don't want to tell him that I sometimes wanted to run away. That's my secret to keep.

"Can I see?" he asks gently, but I shake my head. He seems to understand and doesn't try again. "When it hurt, where you thinking of leaving?"

"How do you know that?" I slap a hand over my mouth as soon as the words have left my lips. I shouldn't be talking so much. I need to keep my secrets close. They're the enemy, they've imprisoned my people. I shouldn't be talking to him at all. I should be running away at the earliest opportunity, as soon as I'm strong enough to walk. I tried yesterday, hoping to reach the little bathroom on the other side of the room, but I barely even managed to sit up.

"We found Andros's diaries. He wrote a long entry on the day he burned that anklet into your skin. The way he describes it... let's just say it made my stomach turn. I'm so sorry for what he did to you."

"I deserved it," I mutter automatically.

"I don't think anyone deserves something like that," he says softly. "Especially because he said that he was planning to give you more."

Shock runs through my body and suddenly, my ankle erupts into pain.

"More?" I whisper.

"After the sinner incident, he ordered a bracelet made with that word. He planned to give it to you soon, but the ascension preparations distracted him."

I take a deep breath, steadying myself. A bracelet. He would have melted it into my wrist, forever marking me as the sinner I am.

"Why?" I ask quietly, hugging myself to hide my wrists under my armpits. "What did I do to deserve that?"

Quentin looks as if he's about to reach out, but then folds his hands on his lap again. "Nothing. He was a sadistic bastard who used his faith to justify what he did. You did nothing wrong, Laya, not ever. You didn't deserve any of it, none of the punishments, none of the ways he treated you. He took away your freedom and made you his-"

"No. He's the Prophet," I tell him, anger bubbling up in me. "He fulfils the Angel's wishes. He always said how he didn't like doing it, but that he had to. He even stayed behind to help us all reach ascension even though he was ready for it. He's a generous, wise leader."

I'm breathing heavily and a headache is spreading behind my temples. It's all too much.

"I want to be back there. I need him, I need my home. I need the Angel. Please, I want to go back." My voice has turned into a whisper, a plea.

This time, he really reaches out and puts a hand on my shoulder. I flinch back. Men aren't allowed to touch women like that. I glare at him and he pulls back, nodding to himself.

"Sorry, I forgot."

How can he forget one of the most essential rules? He's lived with us, he should know. No contact between men and women. Even now, I should tell him to leave. I'm such a hypocrite, letting him talk to me while no other woman is present.

"I come from a family where we do a lot of hugging and touching," he explains. "My parents would be hand in hand pretty much wherever we'd go. I grew up with three sisters, so being around women and treating them like siblings is normal for me. It was very strange living in your community where men and women are separated."

"It's the rule."

"I know. But you're outside of that system now, and rules are different here. You'll have to get used to seeing men and women together again. We're going to try and make the transition as gentle for you as possible, though. We're on your side, Laya, all three of us."

He frowns for a moment. "By the way, what do you want us to call you? Laya or-"

"Laya," I interrupt him before he can use my birth name. I discarded that one when I met Andros and became part of the Angel's flock. Using it now seems like sacrilege.

"Okay then, Laya." He looks at his watch. "I need to go, but Leek will come to visit tomorrow. We thought it would be best for you to chat to all three of us while you're still here."

"Why?"

"We're the ones who're going to look after you. We'll be with you from now until the trial."

Sixteen

This time, the nurse removes the dressings without putting new ones on. I feel much stronger as well, and the thought of leaving the hospital is ticking through my mind. Leaving without them, the three men tasked with protecting me. I don't need protection. I'll find a quiet place to live in peace until Andros and the others are released. Then, everything can go back to how it was before the new men arrived. I wish they'd never come.

I slowly sit up and the nurse puffs up a pillow before sliding it behind my back. Black spots dance in front of my eyes for a second, but when they disappear, I smile. I'm sitting and I'm no longer covered in bandages. Things are improving, but the best thing is yet to come: there's a brownie waiting for me on the small table beside my bed. I saved it for later, and I think now it's time to enjoy that chocolaty goodness. I breathe in deeply and my smile widens. Chocolate smell is the best, almost better than the taste.

I take a tentative bite, but before I can even swallow it,

the door bursts open and two men run in. Leek looks around the room as if he's expecting someone else to be there, while Andrew hurries to my side, beginning to detach cables from the machines without a word.

"We need to go," Leek says, his voice full of alarm and urgency. "No time to explain, but we need to get you out of here right now."

I clench my fist around the brownie that was supposed to be this afternoon's treat. It's worthless now. They've destroyed yet another day for me.

I shriek when Martin, no, Andrew pulls out the cannula from my wrist without warning. He puts some gauze on top of it. "Press that on it," he instructs me brusquely before continuing to free me from the monitors.

"What's going on?" I ask weakly, but all I get is a grunted "later" from Leek. He's rolled a wheelchair closer to the bed and without a word, Andrew lifts me up and puts me on it.

"You can't do that," I complain, but I'm too weak to fight them. Leek wraps a thick blanket around me, and off we go, out of the room, with Andrew wheeling me along the hospital corridor towards an elevator. "Are you kidnapping me?"

Leek chuckles, the first positive sound those two have made since they stormed into my room. "In a way. Don't worry, we're not the bad guys. We'll explain everything once we're in a secure location."

"Secure location sounds a lot like kidnapping," I mutter under my breath, but the sound of the elevator doors opening camouflages the sound. Andrew wheels me in and we take the lift down to the lowest level, the car park.

"You took your sweet time," Quentin greets us as soon as we step, or in my case roll, out of the elevator. He's standing in front of a strategically parked van which is covered in advertising for an office cleaning company. "Hi Laya, good to see you again," he says to me and grins. "Are you ready to go to your new home?"

"No," I grumble. "I'm being kidnapped."

"They've not told you anything?"

"We had to be quick about it," Leek defends the pair still standing behind me. "They could be here any minute."

Quentin nods and opens the back of the van. "Andrew, you're in the back with her. Leek's with me."

"Sorry about this," Andrew whispers and gently lifts me, pressing me against his chest. "I know you don't like being touched."

It's nice of him to finally notice, but that doesn't make it any better. My cheek rubs against his shirt and his scent fills my nostrils, so very different from the sickeningly sweet smell that Andros left behind whenever he visited me. I think I've learned to associate touch with the Prophet and the pain that usually followed it.

The doctor carries me into the van and sits me back down on one of the two car seats mounted to the wall. He puts a seat belt around me, and by now, I'm so weak that it's the only thing holding me up. I don't want them to see my weakness, so I keep my head as straight as possible and continue to glare at them.

Quentin folds the wheelchair and attaches it to the wall opposite with some velcro straps. "All set?" he asks and Andrew nods.

"Yes, let's get out of here."

. . .

Five minutes into the journey, I can't hold myself upright any longer and slump to the right, away from Andrew.

"Laya?" he asks, releasing his seat belt and jumping out of his seat so he can kneel in front of me. "What's wrong?"

He takes my wrist and feels my pulse. It's a comforting gesture, even though it means that he's touching me. "We need to lie you down," he announces, but he keeps his hand on my wrist, his thumb gently stroking my skin. I close my eyes and relax into the touch, so against what I should be doing, but I'm too exhausted to even care. All I want is to feel safe.

Seventeen

'm no longer in hospital. I'm no longer on my old shoddy bed back home either. No, I'm on a warm, soft mattress that moulds around me, hugging me gently. I slowly open my eyes, blinking a few times to get rid of the glue keeping my eyelids stuck together.

It's an unfamiliar room, not very big, but furnished in bright and warm colours that make it seem bigger than it is. There's no window, but a large poster of a window frame looking out to a tropical beach is in its place. Very eighties style, if you ask me, but I guess it's better than no window at all.

I sit up slowly, ignoring the feeling that I'm about to faint. I'm not going to do that. I'm going to be strong. I know how to deal with a painful and weak body, and this is no different. May the Angel help me and be by my side.

There's a small table to my right, more a pedestal than an actual bedside table. There's a tiny brass bell on it, and a note. I pick up the piece of paper first.

Ring when you're awake.

It's the same writing as on the notes I got back in the community. I'm torn inside. On one hand, they helped me, gave me food and hope, but on the other hand, they lied to me the entire time. They lied to everyone, pretending they were someone they're not. Now that I know their real identity, or at least parts of it, those little gestures seem different. Maybe they just wanted to gain my trust. Maybe Andrew only came into my house to plant that bug. And worst of all: they almost let me die just so they could arrest Andros while he was committing a crime.

But still... they were kind to me, and I don't think that was all an act. I'm pretty good at reading people, and I didn't see deceit in their eyes when they talked to me. Yes, they were hiding something, but it wasn't malicious. At one point, I thought that we might become friends after ascension. In another life, I would have loved to get to know them further.

I don't really have a choice, do I? I can't run, I'm far too weak for that. As long as I stay cautious and don't let them close, I should be okay.

I nod in determination and ring the little bell. It's a beautiful, clear sound that reverberates through my bones as the vibrations travel up my arm. I put it down and listen to the echo of the bell and for whatever might follow. Sure enough, there are footsteps in the distance, approaching quickly. A moment later, the door flies open and Andrew steps inside.

"Typical, I leave for ten minutes to get some food, and that's when you wake up."

He grins and walks to my side, sitting down on the bed.

He's careful not to get too close though, and he keeps his hands on his lap.

"How are you?" he asks, his grin disappearing slightly. "We'd thought you were feeling better than you were, and I didn't expect you to crash like you did. I had to give you another IV." He points to a drip stand in the corner behind my bed, an empty plastic bag hanging from its hook.

"I'm fine, I think," I reply quietly. I lift my hand to look at the new cannula that's still embedded in the top of my hand. "Can you remove this?"

He nods and puts on some gloves from his pocket.

"Do you always carry gloves on you?"

He smirks. "We had a prof at university who told us to always carry a pair with us. You never know whether you might come upon an accident or need to entertain a child."

"A child?"

"I'll show you in a moment." He expertly removes the cannula and dresses the wound. His touch is light, careful this time. When he's discarded the needle into a metal bowl at his feet, he grins and blows air into one of the gloves, then ties a knot at the end as if it's a balloon. He takes a pen from his chest pocket and draws something on it, then turns it around and wiggles it in front of my face. "Here you go, an elephant for you."

I can't help but laugh. The thumb part of the glove has turned into an elephant trunk, and he's drawn two eyes and enormous ears on it.

He smiles at me and his eyes light up. "I could have turned it into a cockerel as well, but my brother's children always prefer the elephant."

"You're an uncle?"

"Yes, I've got two nephews. They're twins and quite a handful. I'm glad I get to be the nice uncle who treats them rather than the dad who has to deal with all the discipline and making sure they grow up being nice young men. I much prefer the fun side, at least until I have kids of my own."

I have so many other questions I want to ask, but it isn't proper. I shouldn't be asking for his life before... wait. We're back in his old life. I can't apply the normal rules anymore. I could ask him anything, but it's wrong. There's a reason why that rule was in place. We need to live in the present and prepare for the future, Andros always said. The past is gone and useless.

I swallow my questions about Andrew and look around the room again. "Where are we?"

"A safe place." His smile has slipped a little.

"Where?"

"A house just outside the city." He's being deliberately vague and it's making me angry. First, they kidnap me, and then they refuse to tell me where I am?

"Which city?" I ask, glaring at him.

"You're safe here," is all he says.

"I was safe before!" I sit up a bit more so I can look him straight in the eyes. "I was safe and you took all of that from me! I had my family before, my people, my husband, and now I'm here with three strangers who won't tell me anything! How is that supposed to be better?"

He looks at the bed, evading my gaze. "We'll explain everything soon. Quentin is in a meeting with our superior just now and once he's back, we'll know how much we're allowed to tell you."

"Allowed? So if that boss orders you not to tell me anything, you'll do that?"

He grimaces. "Orders are orders. I may have full authority when it comes to medical matters, but we do have people in charge who usually have the bigger picture and know what's sensible. Sure, they're wrong sometimes, and we have been known to disregard orders occasionally, but in this case, we're going to listen."

His voice has turned stern, as if to make sure that there's no point in arguing with him.

I lean back against the soft pillow behind me. The room is no longer looking as friendly as when I first woke up.

"So what am I?" I ask grimly. "Your prisoner?"

Finally he looks up at me again, anguish reflected on his face. "Don't ever think that. We're here to protect you. I can't tell you everything, but know that there are people out there who want to hurt you. To keep you safe, we need you to stay with us for now, inside, until we've sorted out a new identity for you. It's not a quick process, and we'll have to get you used to life in the normal world again. Right now, it would be too overwhelming, which would make it easy for them to spot you."

"Them?"

He sighs. "I've said too much already. I'm sorry, Laya, Quentin will hopefully be back soon and then we can have a proper conversation. Until then, can I get you anything? Something to read? Food?"

I shake my head and close my eyes, making it very obvious that I want to be left alone.

"Sleep some more," he says softly and gets up from his chair. "I'll wake you when there's news."

This time, I do as he asks.

The smell of fresh bread wakes me. For a tiny moment, I think I'm back home, but far too soon my memories return and I remember all that's happened. The little bell is still on the table next to me, and this time, I ring it more forcefully.

"On my way!" a man shouts from somewhere, maybe a few rooms away from my own. While I wait, I try and sit up, and it works surprisingly well. I'm a little stronger and wiggling around until I find a better position feels easy. Maybe I'll be able to get up later and walk around. I could do with a toilet break.

Someone knocks on the door. How polite. I guess they're now trying to make me feel less like a prisoner.

"Come in," I call out and Leek enters, carrying a plate with two giant slabs of bread. I remember the day I got a similar sandwich and shiver.

"I thought you might be hungry," he says, but he continues to stand in the doorway as if he's not quite sure how to act around me.

I give him a slight smile to bridge the tension. "It smells good."

He grins. "This baking stuff is really growing on me. Quentin even bought me a Mary Berry recipe book, although I'm not sure if that was a joke or not." He shrugs. "Want some?"

I nod and he comes closer, handing me the plate. There's enough bread on there for three people. One of the slices has been covered in a thick layer of butter and a sprinkle of parsley, while the other is drowning under a mountain of cheese. He either has no idea of how much people can eat, or he's simply overdoing it out of nervosity.

"Can I sit down for a bit?" he asks, but I'm already munching away on the delicious bread. The crust is perfectly crunchy, but the middle is soft and squishy.

He takes a seat and watches me eat.

"It's delicious," I say once I've swallowed. "You're really good at this."

He smiles widely. "I'm not just the muscle."

"The muscle?" I take another bite while I await his explanation.

"That's what they call me. Quentin's the brain, Drew's the deft hands and I'm the muscle. We make a good team, most of the time."

"What exactly is it that you do?"

He huffs. "I probably shouldn't be telling you this, but to be honest, I couldn't care less. Ever heard of SOCA?"

I shake my head, the bread forgotten.

"Serious Organised Crime Agency. We deal with all the serious stuff happening here in Scotland. Drugs, forced prostitution, human trafficking, you name it. We're part of the police, but under the direct command of the government, which also means that not all of us are originally police officers. I used to be special forces and Andrew used to work in war zones for Médecins Sans Frontières."

"What about Quentin?" I ask, almost calling him Owen by mistake. It's going to take a little more time to get used to the new names.

"He's proper police. Forensic psychologist and profiler. He's far cleverer than he lets on."

I put the bread down, suddenly feeling queasy. "Does that mean he's analysing me? Profiling me? Like a criminal?"

To my surprise, Leek grins. "You, me, everyone. I don't think he can control it. He's trying to understand everyone he meets, and when he can't, he becomes a little obsessed. I think he's going to be very annoyed that he'll miss out on interrogating Andros."

I go over our last conversation again. How much of that was him being a psychologist? How much was him, the person? Or are the two intertwined? Does it matter? In the end, I've got no secrets he could expose. My weaknesses are drawn on my back in large, puckered scars.

Eighteen

The sound of the doorbell interrupts our conversation. Two short rings, two long, another short one.

"That's Quentin," Leek announces, already on his way out of the room. "Don't worry, we'll come join you here in a moment. Milk and sugar?"

"Huh?"

"I'm making tea, I always make tea for our meetings. Milk? Sugar?"

"No, thanks," I mutter. I haven't drunk tea since I moved into the community. Drinks that have an effect on the mind were forbidden: tea, coffee, alcohol, sugary drinks. We mainly stuck to water, and occasionally some fruit juice on special occasions.

He leaves. I'm alone again, with a very full bladder. There must be a bathroom nearby. Question is, will I make it there on my own?

Only one way to find out. I push the blanket off me, which takes a surprising amount of effort. I'm still weaker than I thought. It's only now that I notice that I'm wearing a different pair of pyjamas than what I wore in hospital. Someone's changed my clothes. One of the men has changed my clothes. They undressed me without my permission, without my knowledge. Bile rises up in my throat when I imagine how they could have looked at my naked body. Men can't be trusted. The only time men and women should talk and touch is when they're married. That's the rule. This goes against everything I know and it makes me physically sick. I need to get away from them.

I slide my legs off the bed and sit there for a moment, waiting for my head to stop spinning. When it finally does, I stand, holding onto the bed just in case. My legs are shaking, but I manage to stay on my feet. That's a good start.

I take a deep breath and let go of the bed. The door isn't that far, only a few steps. I can do this. I walk, no, I stagger towards it, my arms outstretched in case I fall. My head is spinning and my vision is flaky, but I make it. I cling to the door handle for support, but I know I need to be quick about it. The men will probably return any moment now, and I want to do this without them. I want to preserve my last bit of dignity.

I open the door as quietly as I can, glad it's not one of the squeaky doors we had in the village. Now, where to next? There are doors to both sides of the corridor, and none of them look as if they lead to a bathroom. Signs would be helpful. There are three doors to my right and two to my left, so I choose to turn right. The chances are higher there.

I'm halfway down the corridor when I stumble over a

fold in the carpet. I'm not fast enough to find my balance and I fall to the ground like a sack of potatoes. Yes, that's what I feel like. A stupid, weak sack of potatoes that can't do anything by itself.

I roll onto my side and manage to sit up, but everything is going black and then bright again, my vision flickering and turning. I'm feeling nauseous, but I can't stop now. I need to get to the bathroom or there will be an accident. I couldn't stand that humiliation.

"What the fuck are you doing there?"

The beeping in my ears is almost drowning out Andrew's voice. I've been discovered.

"Bathroom," I say weakly, leaning against the wall to stop the shaking.

He squats down in front of me, looking at me sternly. "That's why you've got the bell. You need something, you ring it. You could have hurt yourself."

I let that sentence reverberate in my mind for a moment, then I laugh. I laugh and giggle and for some reason, tears are beginning to flow down my cheeks.

Andrew stares at me in confusion. "What's so funny?"

"I could have got hurt," I snort between bouts of laughter.

His frown is growing more concerned. "Did you hit your head?"

"Hurt!" I continue to laugh. "I got hurt so often, and now a walk to the bathroom could have hurt me?"

He doesn't seem to see the joke, which makes me laugh even harder.

"Is it alright if I carry you?" he asks, and my laughter

immediately stops. He wants to touch me again. It's wrong, so wrong.

I shake my head, glowering at him.

He sighs. "Wheelchair it is. Stay here, don't move."

I laugh again. As if I could.

He helps me into the large bathroom, but then he leaves me alone to do my business. Thank the Angel for that small mercy. When I'm done, I splatter some water into my face, looking into the mirror for the first time in... well, ages. I've seen my reflection in water sometimes, or in the smooth metal of pots in the kitchen, but this mirror shows the ugly truth. My cheeks are gaunt and pale, not as round as I remember them. A thin layer of downy hair covers my scalp, broken by small scars where I cut myself in the past. I'll have to ask for a razor soon. My eyes are the worst though. They don't look like me. They're surrounded by grey shadows and there's no spark. They're devoid of life. Blank. Dead.

I stumble backwards and fall into the wheelchair. For how long have I looked this way? Only since the failed ascension? Or longer? Is that why the three men gave me food? To try and make me look less starved and dead?

I'm not a vain person, not at all. But I have dignity, and the woman in the mirror doesn't look dignified. She doesn't even look human.

"Are you done?" Andrew calls from outside, but I can't answer. There's a lump in my throat that's forecasting more tears. I just want to go to bed, curl up and cry.

Of course, I rarely get what I want. I knock against the door and let Andrew wheel me back to my room. The others are waiting there for us. They've brought some chairs and a low table that's covered in files and paper. And tea, four large mugs.

Andrew helps me back into bed. I think he makes sure to touch me as little as possible, but right now, I don't care. The image of my own dead eyes flashes through my mind whenever I blink. This is what they see when they look at me. Not the Laya I am inside. The frail Laya I'm on the outside. I need to change that. I don't want to look as weak as I feel.

When I'm seated comfortably, Andrew holds out his hand. There's four pills on it, three round ones and one long one with what looks like tiny pearls inside.

"Vitamins," he explains. "You're malnourished."

I shake my head. "I don't take man-made medicine like that."

"It's the same stuff you find in fruit and vegetables," he says calmly. "Just concentrated to make it easier to get a large amount of it. If you'd prefer to eat at least ten apples a day, go ahead."

"If you take them, I'll make brownies," Leek suggests with a grin.

"What?"

He smiles. "You were holding one when we came to the hospital. I assumed you liked them?"

I shrug. "I think so, it's a long time since I've had cake."

"Good." Leek winks at me and points at the vitamin pills. "Do we have a deal?"

If I relax this one rule, it will be easy to relax other ones as well. I'll become a sinner, just like Andros always told me. I need to stay strong. One step towards sin can set you on a road you can't leave. But... brownies. And Andrew said that it's basically like eating lots of apples. I'd rather eat brownies than apples. Both are good, both are sweet, but after smelling that chocolatey scent yesterday...

I take the pills and swallow them. I'm a sinner already, and right now, I'm in an environment bursting with sin. I will have to adapt to survive, or I'll never be able to return to my home. It's just until the others are released and we can go back to our life of prayer and devotion.

"Can I have a statue of the Angel?" I blurt out before I can stop myself. All three of them look at me strangely.

"I think they confiscated a lot of people's belongings in the compound, but I'll see what I can do," Quentin promises after a long pause, and begins to type something into his phone. Mobiles have changed a lot since I left society. His is big and shiny, with a large screen and almost no buttons. At the beginning, I missed technology, especially my trusted laptop, but I got used to it pretty quickly. We didn't communicate with people outside of our group, so we didn't have use for phones and the such.

"Thank you." Leek hands me a mug, the only one where the tea is dark brown rather than milky. I take a sip and almost burn my tongue. I giggle. Somehow, I'm getting hurt in all sorts of new ways today.

"So, what's going on?" Andrews asks Quentin. "Did they catch them?"

"No, but you were right, they tried to get into the hospital. One of our officers almost caught them, but they got away before reinforcements arrived. But there's some bad news." He shoots me a cautious glance, as if to assess whether I'll be able to handle it.

"Maybe start from the beginning," Leek suggests.

Quentin nods. "Yes, I'm allowed to do that now. Laya, when you joined Andros and the others, did he make you sign something? A contract, perhaps?"

I think back to when we first moved to the village. It's so long ago now, but I dimly remember how we all signed a sheet of paper. "Yes, to promise that we'd give up all our worldly belongings and fully concentrate on our new life in servitude to the Angel."

He nods again and rummages on the table until he finds a sheet of paper. "This one?" He hands it to me and I skim it.

"Yes, I think so."

He sighs softly. "I'm not quite sure how to start. When Andros founded the Angel's flock, he set it up as a company. Not as a charity, which would have made sense, but as a business. There's a clause in the contract you all signed that states that if you die, all your money and everything you still own will pass over to him. Which means that if all sixty people die, he gets a shitload of money. Not just him, the entire company."

I shake my head in confusion. This can't be true, this isn't real. They're trying to turn me away from Andros and the light. "No, that doesn't make sense. He was going to ascend as well, so what use would that money be?"

Quentin's expression softens even further. "We're not sure if he was ever going to join you in death," he tells me and my world shatters.

Nineteen

"But he's the Prophet! He was going to lead us into Paradise! He's the one who's been talking to the Angel, who's been guided by the divine. Andros was going to ascend, trust me."

They don't look convinced, but also don't seem to argue with me.

"Even if he was going to join you," Quentin continues, "there are other people involved. The business he founded is shady, and there are loans he took to have the money to build your compound. If he dies as well, that money will go to those people, so now they're very interested in getting rid of everyone involved, including you."

"Me? But I didn't even have much money! A few hundred in the bank, but nothing that would warrant anyone wanting to kill me!" I run my hands over my shorn scalp, feeling the soft hair that's growing there again.

"You don't know?" Leek asks, confusion all over his face. "Didn't he tell you?"

"Tell me what?" By now I'm exasperated and tears are threatening to flow again. Everything is spiralling out of control and the ground beneath my feet is disintegrating. I'm about to fall, and once I do, there's nothing to catch me.

"Your mother died a year ago and left you a substantial amount. I'm so sorry, Laya."

I just stare at him, my mind trying to catch up unsuccessfully. "Money? My mum? She never had any money."

Quentin grimaces. "She wrote a book after you joined Andros. 'My Daughter, the Cultist'. It became quite successful. It's ironic how that book money is now endangering you."

"Wait, but there must be some kind of law that means they can't get the money if I'm murdered?"

"Not if they aren't officially involved. And so far, they seem to try and make it look like suicides."

A shiver runs over my skin when I realise what that means. "So far? Someone's died?"

"It's not clear yet whether it was murder or suicide-"

"Who?" I interrupt.

"Eamon and his wife. Eamon was the one with the biggest wealth, so it would make sense-"

"He was the Prophet's second in command," I interrupt again. "Of course he'd choose ascension. He's a role model for all of us. We should all be following his example."

Quentin shoots me a sharp look. "You're not thinking of doing that, are you?"

I avert my eyes. Am I? Do I still want to ascend? In a way, I want to be with the Angel. This new world is scary and frightening, and I don't think I'll ever fit in. If I still had the community, it would be different. We could continue to live as before, striving for the perfect devoted life. But here, in the outside world, it's so hard to stick to the rules. I'd rather ascend now than become a sinner and forego any chance of ever joining the Angel in Paradise.

"I'm putting you on suicide watch," Quentin announces when I don't reply. "One of us will be with you at all times. I'm sorry to have to do that, but we're here to protect you, both from others and from yourself."

"I wouldn't do it," I protest feebly, but I think we both know that's a lie. Ascension seems more and more like the only solution. With Andros in prison, I might be able to spend a few years, decades even, in Paradise without him. I could be happy. I feel my lips twitch into a smile when I think of the Angel's light.

"Leek, find a bed that'll fit into this room. We'll take shifts."

"You can't do that," I protest, "I've got rights."

"It's for your own good," Andrew tries to explain, but I cut him off.

"I know what's best for me. You're just trying to control me. How is that any different from Andros? At least there I had the Angel and our prayers. Here I have nothing, only chaos."

"Is that why you joined? To have structure rather than chaos?" Leek asks calmly.

"Are you the therapist now?" I shoot back, getting angrier by the minute. "Get out."

I have no idea from where I take the courage to talk to them like that, but it feels good. They can't tell me what to do. They're not acting on behalf of the Angel. I follow his rules, gladly, but these men's words don't matter. Nothing in this world matters.

"One of us will have to stay," Leek says, almost sadly. "Who would you prefer?"

I put my still full mug on the bedside table and turn in the bed until I'm facing away from them. I don't want any of them here. I just want to be alone.

"I'll stay," Andrew says in his soft, careful voice. "In case there's any medical problems."

Chairs are being pushed back and two pairs of footsteps head towards the door. "I'll find a bed," Leek promises from afar. I don't want him to, but it seems like I don't have a voice in any of this. They just do what they want, all under the guise of protecting me.

"Are you feeling alright? Any pain?" Andrew asks but I ignore him. Strangely enough, there's no pain at all. I don't think I've ever been pain-free, at least it feels that way. I'm still weak, but he's said that I will grow stronger soon once the last of the poison has left my body.

Their words are echoing around my head. Money. Contracts. People wanting to kill us. Me. My mum, dead. My sweet, crazy mother. Andros told me about my father dying in a car accident, but why didn't he mention my mum? Maybe he didn't know. Maybe nobody told him.

"How did she die?" I whisper, hoping that he'll know what I mean.

"An aneurism. It was quick, probably painless. I think your aunt tried to contact the cult, but nobody ever got back to her. I think she'd probably be glad to hear from you. She's been part of the police investigation after your mother died."

"What? Why would she be involved?"

"When nobody answered her letters, she drove to the compound. She never got into the village, she was stopped before she got there. She did see more than she should have, though. Outside the village, close to where she parked her car, she saw Andros and a woman. That villager wasn't there voluntarily. He was hitting her and doing much worse. Your aunt drove off and informed the police. She was scared that it hadn't just been an isolated incident, that all of the women were treated that way."

He pauses for a moment, but I don't say anything.

"Do you want her to visit? I could arrange for her to come here, if you want. It might be nice for you to see a familiar face."

I try and remember my aunt. I never knew her that well. My mum's sister had been a bit of a hippie, always travelling to distant places. The last time I saw her must have been several years before I even met Andros. Ten years ago, probably. I don't think I'd call her a familiar face.

"No, thanks."

Don't get attached to people outside of the community. That's why we settled so far away from other villages and towns. Less temptation to mingle with non-believers.

"That's fine. Let me know when you change your mind."

He falls silent again and leaves me to my thoughts. I almost wish he didn't. My mind is chaos and I feel like I'm being torn apart in different directions. I'm at a fork in the road, but it's not me who chooses where to turn. It's other people choosing for me, and I'm hating it. If they pull any more, I'm going to rip apart.

I need to find control over my life again. I need to make them stop choosing for me.

Twenty

My night is restless. I've slept too much the day before, and the presence of Andrew in the room is making me uncomfortable. I can hear him breathe, and I know he's awake. I can tell apart the breathing rhythm of someone who's asleep and someone who isn't. I'm not sure he knows that I'm not sleeping either, but he doesn't say anything.

I stare at the ceiling for most of the night, trying to sleep but at the same trying not to. I'm afraid of the nightmares lurking in the shadows.

Because there are no windows, I'm relying on someone to come and tell me that it's morning. There's no clock anywhere, and I don't own a watch. I'm used to waking up when the sun rises, or when the morning bell rings on the rare occasions that I don't wake by myself. Here, I have neither.

At some point, I can't stifle my impatience any longer. "What time is it?" I ask into the darkness.

A light flashes for a moment, then Andrew yawns loudly. "Five in the morning. Can't sleep?"

"You're not sleeping either," I counter and he chuckles.

"I'm not supposed to. Shall I switch on the light?"

I nod before I realise he can't see it. "Yes, please."

He gets up from his bed and walks to the door. I squeeze my eyes shut when he switches on the light, but it's better than the darkness.

"What shall we do?" He smiles at me. "I'm pretty sure the others are still sleeping. Leek especially, he likes to sleep in."

"You could leave?" I suggest and his smile widens.

"Not happening, but you know that. Not until Quentin tells us that it's fine. He's the expert."

"Is he the one in charge?"

He nods. "Yeah, he's the most senior in the team. When it comes to medical matters, they usually let me make the decisions, but he's the one reporting to our superiors. He actually likes doing paperwork, so I don't have a problem with that." He shrugs light-heartedly. "I think he missed doing it while we were undercover. If we'd stayed longer, he would have probably asked if he could help out in the office."

"How long were you planning to stay?"

"As long as it took to gather enough evidence. It was hard though, seeing how everyone's medical needs were so blatantly ignored. When that woman died in childbirth, that was the moment I was closest to calling in the cavalry and getting you all out of there. It was negligence that killed her and her baby. I'm not sure I could have saved them, but proper medical care could have probably prevented it from happening in the first place. Anyway, soon after, we heard more about ascension and the decision was made that we'd stay and observe some more, rather than intervene immediately."

He sighs deeply. "I've been undercover before, but I've never seen anything like it. The way you were treated, the way Andros hurt you every night... Any other situation and we'd have got you out of there on day one, but we needed to weigh up the needs of the individual against the needs of the entire community."

He looks pained as he says it, as if he didn't agree when that decision was made. "We probably shouldn't have sent you messages, it could have exposed us, but after the first you had that spark in your eyes, for the first time since we'd arrived. I think it was hope."

The roll with the hidden message. You'll be safe soon, that's what it said. It made my ankle hurt, but I remember the feeling of warmth that spread through my stomach at the thought of someone looking out for me. In retrospective, it all makes sense. They weren't allowed to help me in other ways, so they tried to keep up my hope. I guess it worked, in a way.

"Thank you," I mutter, hoping that he'll understand what I mean.

"I'm just glad you never showed them to Andros. We were worried, at the beginning, because we didn't know how close the two of you were. But after he made you run across the square naked, it was pretty clear that he was mistreating you."

"Let's not talk about that."

"Okay." He smiles at me. "But if you ever want to talk, I'm here. I'll always listen."

We stay in silence after that, but it's a comfortable silence now. I actually manage to fall asleep for a bit, until Leek comes in with a large tray, followed by Quentin.

"Breakfast," he calls cheerily, balancing the tray until Andrew makes space on his bed for it. The table from yesterday has disappeared to make space for the camping bed. "I made scones. I don't have clotted cream, but I guess butter and jam will do."

Andrew snickers. "You know the rest of us will never cook again, now that we know how good you are at it."

"Baking isn't cooking," Leek laughs. "Just because I can make dough doesn't mean that I have any idea how the hob works. I can just about figure out the knobs on the oven. At least this kitchen isn't as complicated as the last one."

I peek up. "You don't actually live here?"

"Here?" Quentin laughs. "No, this is just a safe house used for witness protection. We've stayed in a few of those, and this is one of the better ones. Usually it's men we protect, but you're a special case. Oh, that reminds me, our boss asked whether you would like her to assign a female agent to our team?"

Another person to spy on me? No thanks. I shake my head and grab one of the scones to avoid having to answer. Leek has put a thick layer of butter on it, covered in a just as thick dollop of strawberry jam. I think one of them will be enough to keep me full all day.

"Those are great," Quentin says, his mouth still full.

Someone should tell him that it's not polite to speak while eating. "You should change your job."

Leek chuckles. "No thanks. That would make my name even more awkward. A baker called Leek, imagine if I started to make vegetable pies."

Even I have to smile at that. "I quite liked you being Noran," I tell him. "It suited you."

He shrugs. "I have no idea what that name even meant. I'd hate having to spell it whenever someone needed to write my name down."

"You have to spell your current name," Andrew points out with a grin. "Leek? Like the vegetable or leak like the hole in the pipe?" He says it in a voice which is probably supposed to resemble a call centre agent.

"Shut it and eat your scone," Leek mutters but he's still smiling. This is the first time I see them interact like that. When they took me from the hospital, they were all business and there was no time for banter. Same yesterday when they explained why I had to be protected. Today, they're relaxed. I like this side of them. They're a bit like a family. I guess if they work together day and night, they have to be friends or at least like each other.

"How long have you been a team?" I ask when I've finished the scone and licked the last crumbs from my fingers.

The men look at each other. "Five years, I think?" Quentin asks and the others nod. He laughs. "I can't believe I've put up with you two for so long."

"Watch it or I'll put some salt in your next scone," Leek threatens with a playful frown.

"We're like brothers by now," Andrew adds.

"Sometimes we fight, sometimes we laugh, sometimes we don't want to be together. But all in all, we're a good team."

"The best," Leek says with a wink.

I smile at his enthusiasm. He does that winking thing in a way that makes it endearing rather than cheesy.

"What did you work on before investigating us?" I ask, trying not to sound bitter about the second part.

"We can't tell you," Quentin says at the same time as Andrew says, "drug cartel". The psychologist shoots him a forceful look. "We don't talk about our missions."

Andrew holds up his hands in defeat. "Okay, we don't talk about how we've investigated drug cartels, and the pornography ring before that, and the pimp before that, and..."

"Shut it," Quentin growls but he's smiling. They're back to their banter. We never had conversations like that in the village. It was always about the Angel and how to be better people. We tried not to talk about personal things, and certainly not about our jobs and lives before we found the Angel. It was a life with a lot less laughter than the men here seem to be leading, despite the seriousness of their work. I kind of like it. Maybe I can learn to do the same. Maybe I can become their friend.

When we're done with breakfast, Leek clears up and Andrew mutters something about taking a shower. They leave me with Quentin and I'm sure it's on purpose.

He's the hardest of them to read. Leek is large and muscly, but is also caring and has a good sense of humour. Andrew can be serious, but he's kind at heart, even though he likes to swear. Quentin though... I don't know. He was interested and nice back in the community when he asked me questions about the Prophet's words, but then he was so serious and cold yesterday. His light blue eyes are piercing enough to reach into my soul, break the barriers around my secrets and pull them all into the light.

"I'm sorry we're having to do this," he says as soon as the others are gone and he's taken a seat again. "Curtailing your freedom like that really isn't something I want to do."

I frown at him. Is he trying to lull me into a false sense of security around him?

"I just want to make sure you're safe. From others and from yourself. You've been caged and mistreated for years in that place, and I want you to have the chance to live again. You don't smile a lot, but when you do, it's beautiful. Like sunshine on a cloudy day. I want to help you push away the clouds and leave only the sun behind."

He shrugs. "Sorry for that awful metaphor. There's a reason I'm not a poet."

"But that's exactly what ascension is," I tell him excitedly. "All the burdens of humanity gone and all that's left is the bright light of the Angel. Don't you see? We want the same thing. I'm going to smile when I'm there, under his warming care."

His left eye twitches, but he's got it under control immediately. I'm going to have to keep an eye on that. Maybe it's his weak spot, the place where he reveals his emotions.

"Why can't you smile here on Earth, Laya? Why can't you be happy here and then, at the end of a long and fulfilled life, ascend to the Angel? Both could be possible, if you only want it."

I shake my head decisively. "There is no happiness on this world. Just look at everything that's happening. The greed, the violence, the suffering. The Angel is the only way to escape it."

"I'm happy," he says, looking straight into my eyes as if to drive the point home. "And the other two. We're happy together. And all the things you mentioned? Well, we're fighting them. We're working hard to help prevent violence and suffering. Don't you think the Angel would want you to do that? Helping others so they can have a better life? Not by telling them to ascend and have a new life in Paradise, but to make their current life better?"

"Andros always said that the trials we go through on Earth prepare us for ascension," I explain. "Suffering is the road to peace. It's the only way."

"That's what Andros said?"

I nod. "It's in the Prophet's words that he wrote down."

Quentin gets up from his chair. There's something stormy about his expression, as if there's emotion curling underneath the surface, waiting to explode into the light. "I'll be back in a moment."

He leaves me confused, not just because he left so suddenly. Some of what he said made sense, and I feel like I don't have the right words to explain why it doesn't.

He's back after only a minute or so, carrying a large stack of folders.

"The originals are with the investigation team, but I got some copies." He drops them on the camping bed and picks up the top folder. "They're his diaries. Andros's diaries. We only have the ones from the last two years, but they're combing the compound to see if they can find any others. They're a fascinating read, believe me. Terrifying, actually."

I knew that Andros wrote a diary, but I never read any of them. He kept them locked away and I would never have dreamed of trying to get access to them. He shared all the visions and dreams the Angel sent him, but he kept diaries for his personal thoughts.

Quentin opens the first page and points at it. "Andros split his daily entry into three different sections: how the community was doing, his own experiences and thoughts, and finally, you."

"Me?" My heart is beginning to beat faster.

"Yes, you. I don't want you to read them, not yet, anyway. They're pretty harrowing, and I've read my fair share of stuff written by psychopaths, believe me. He recounts every single beating he gave you. He describes how you looked before and after, and how you reacted. He even rates them on a scale from one to ten. Then he's got a tick box to note whether he..." He takes a deep breath. "Whether he raped you. But the worst bit is that he has a second scale that shows how close you've come to his ultimate goal."

Shivers are running over my skin and I can't stop my breathing grow faster. "What?"

"It just says one word. Broken. He wanted to break you completely, Laya. That's why he was doing it all. His aim was to take you as a young, confident woman and turn you into a broken slave."

"What?" It's a whisper this time. No. Can't. Too much. Something erupts within me, shattering me into a million pieces, and all I can do is scream and howl and fight against the arms that are embracing me. Pain is flashing over my skin, the pain of a thousand whip lashes, the pain Andros gave me. I see his face, his cruel eyes, his laugh, his lips whispering how I'm his little bird. He's everywhere, I can feel his touch, he's in me, on me, he is me.

My scream turns into a whimper, a sound that barely seems human. There are voices now, other voices, lots of voices, but I don't know if they're real or memories. I'm floating inside the images and sounds of the past, unable to escape them. People, places, emotions. Then, again, always, Andros. His eyes that drew me in at first, and then spit me out again later. So much pain. I clutch whoever is holding me, grateful that I'm not alone.

I stay in his embrace for hours. At some point, I throw up, but he keeps me close, anchoring me to the present. The others come in and leave again, make me drink some water, whisper soothing words. When the pain finally lessens and the images stop flashing in front of my eyes, I fall into deep sleep, a strange feeling of being safe helping keep the nightmares away.

Twenty-One

"Do you think that was wise? It broke her."

Whispered voices in the distance.

"Trust me, I've thought long and hard about it, but better to tell her now and then help her get back to her feet. Doing it in small doses may work for other people, but with her still thinking of suicide, I needed to do something drastic. She's going to need some time to recover, but she's strong."

"That she is. I don't think I would have lasted half as long as she did, and that's with all the training we got. She's special."

"What are we going to do about her request? The Angel statue?"

"I managed to organise us one. We only want her to stop believing that she's inferior and needs to follow Andros's deluded rules, but we don't want to take away her entire belief system. That would be counterproductive at this stage. As long as it's a positive and not self-destructive belief, let's support it."

"Fine by me. I don't think believing in the Angel is necessarily a bad thing. It might give her strength to continue fighting."

The voices disappear and I fall back into my slumber, already starting to forget what I heard.

When I wake up again, I'm wide awake. And thirsty, oh so thirsty. I'm halfway out of bed when I remember that I was ill and don't have my full strength back. I don't want to risk falling again. With a sigh, I ring the little bell on my bedside table.

My head feels strange. Clearer, somehow, as if some kind of fog has been lifted from around my thoughts. I barely remember what happened before I went to sleep. Well, I do remember, but the memories are behind a milky screen which I know I can wipe clean whenever I want. Right now, I don't want to take a closer look. I know that it was bad, very bad, but I feel happier now than I have in ages. Whatever happened is over now. What I do remember is being held, looked after, cared for. I liked that feeling. It wasn't a sexual touch and embrace, but something much deeper.

"You called, milady?"

I didn't even notice Leek entering the room. The door must have been open, or at least not properly shut.

I smile at his choice of words. "I feel quite thirsty. Would it be possible to get a drink, dear sir?" I say it in a posh English accent that would give the Queen a run for her money. "Wait, is the Queen still alive?" I ask as an afterthought.

"Oh yes, alive and ticking. Prince Philip died last year though, but she's soldiering on."

"That's sad."

He shrugs. "He was over ninety. I think that's a pretty good age. Now, tea without milk and sugar?"

I nod. "And do you still have some scones left?"

He smiles. "Tea and scones coming up."

Leek disappears and I'm left grinning to myself. Why am I suddenly so happy? I can't stop smiling. Is it a side effect of the poison, perhaps? Is it affecting my brain?

One scone and a mug of tea later, I'm brimming with energy. I want to do something, anything. First problem though, I don't have any clothes save the pyjamas I'm in.

"Ehm, Leek," I ask, a little embarrassed.

"Yes? Another scone?"

"No, but... I don't have any clothes. As comfortable as these pyjamas are, they're not very... appropriate." Angel, this is embarrassing. Right now, I wish there was a woman here rather than three men.

"I'll find you something," Leek promises. "Does that mean you're ready to leave the bed?"

His eyes lighten up a little.

"I think I'm feeling up to it," I say, surprised by his reaction. "I kind of want to know where I am."

He nods. "I can give you a tour in the wheelchair for now?"

As much as I hate that thing, it's probably for the best.

Better than being carried. Don't let them touch you, a voice in my head calls, but I push it away, behind the milky glass that's keeping me sane.

"Let me just check with Andrew, he's the doctor. I don't want to break you or anything." His smile disappears for a fraction of a second, then it's back.

He leaves and returns a minute later with Andrew in tow. His hair is wet; he must have just taken a shower. I wonder how often I'll be allowed to shower here. Is there a schedule? I make a mental note to ask later. Being in bed for so long has made me sweaty and dirty, but that's not a new feeling.

"I hear you want to get up?" the doctor asks and sits on the edge of my bed. "That's good, I wanted to encourage you to do that anyway. We need to get your body used to moving again. I'll just measure your blood pressure and then we're good to go."

While he does that, I try not to focus on the feel of his cold fingers on my skin. It makes me want to flinch and push him away, but at the same time my brain is telling me that there's nothing to fear.

"Your pulse is a little high," Andrew mutters. I look away, pretty sure it's because I'm reacting badly to his touch. My body is telling me to run.

"I think she doesn't like you touching her," Leek says from the other side of the room. He's leaning against the wall, watching us closely. "She looks like she's about to jump out of bed."

"I can hear you," I tell him, but he's right.

Andrew slides the blood pressure cuff down my arm

and as soon as his fingers leave my skin, the tension in me eases.

"Okay then," he says softly. "Sorry."

I shake my head, feeling bad for him. "It's not your fault. I know you're just doing your job, but it's wrong, men and women touching, and we're not..." I break off, my voice echoing through my head. "I'm aware it's normal for you, but it isn't for me."

"Don't feel bad about it." Andrew smiles but his eyes are sad. "I promise I'm not going to touch you unless it's necessary for medical purposes. Is that alright?"

I nod, grateful but also slightly annoyed at myself. I'm giving them so much trouble. I should try better to fit in. As much as they're imprisoning me, I think they also genuinely want to help me.

"Just because I don't like being touched, doesn't mean that we can't be..." I take a deep breath before saying the next word. Am I making a mistake here? "... friends."

"Friends sounds good," Andrew says, his eyes lighting up. "Very good."

"Your chariot awaits." Leek rolls the wheelchair close enough to the bed so I can get onto it myself. Andrew instructs me to first sit on the bed for a bit to get my circulation used to it, then he lets me stand and walk the two steps to the chair. Surprisingly, my head only spins a little, not enough to make me feel like I'm about to faint. Things are improving. The positive mood I'm in is both unfamiliar and infectious. I'm not sure what to make of it. In a way, I want to run around screaming and hugging everyone, on the other hand I'm terribly scared of it. That's not me. Not calm, demure Laya. It threatens to make me break the rules. Already I'm talking to them as if they're not strangers, and men at that. I even want to be friends with them. If I continue in this direction, I might abandon all my principles and become like the people Andros always warned us about. Sinners and fornicators.

"Let's start with the kitchen," Leek chuckles and begins to wheel me out of the room. "It's the most important place in this flat."

"At least this location has one," Andrew mutters behind me. "The last safe house we stayed in only had a kitchenette with a microwave. Four weeks of eating nothing but microwave meals and the occasional takeaway. We're not allowed to get deliveries, so one of us had to drive ten miles to the nearest pizza place. Dreadful."

I smile at the horror in his voice. "How far is the nearest takeaway from here?"

"Nice try," Leek says with a laugh. "But we can't tell you where you are, not yet. But here you go, the kitchen."

We enter a large, bright room full of marble sideboards and chrome armatures. Whoever chose this kitchen had a lot of money. There's two ovens even, and a table large enough to seat at least eight people. Everything is spotless, but a plate of biscuits in the centre of the table helps make it look like a home that's lived in rather than a kitchen out of a furniture brochure.

"Welcome to Leek's Paradise," Andrew chuckles and walks around the wheelchair so I can see him. "It's come as quite a shock to see him enjoy baking so much, but I won't complain. That chocolate cake last week was delicious. We wanted to bring some to the hospital, but they didn't let us visit at the beginning."

"Why not?" I ask, remembering how he was my first visitor and the only one who got me to wake up from my stupor.

"Procedure." He sighs. "After an undercover mission, they don't like us interacting with the people we investigated, even if they're the victims rather than the perpetrators. It took a lot of persuasion to get them to agree to a visit, and a bit of blackmail to let us be your protectors."

"Having a detailed knowledge of cult victim case studies helped," Quentin chimes in from behind me. "Good to see you up and about, Laya."

He steps into my field of vision. "How are you feeling?"

I shrug. "Weird."

He observes me closely, then nods and smiles. "We should have a chat later, but let's continue the tour. I wouldn't want you to miss out on exploring this glorious place."

"Don't mock the flat," Leek complains. "It could have been a lot worse."

"You're not the one having to share a bedroom with Andrew," Quentin jokes. "He snores."

"I do not," the man in question protests. "Laya can attest to that."

I smile at his attempt to let me take part in the banter. "You never actually slept."

"Which means I didn't snore. Point proven. Now, shall we go on? We still have to show you the living room."

Leek turns us around and wheels me out of the kitchen, but not before grabbing some biscuits from the table and handing me one.

"Trail food," he whispers, already munching on his own. "And proof that I want to be your friend, too."

"Weren't they supposed to be for this afternoon?" Quentin asks with mock anger.

"Just testing. We wouldn't want to give Mrs M something that doesn't taste good."

"Who?" Are we getting a visitor? I'm not sure how I feel about that. For now, I like not having to interact with other people; people who aren't part of the Angel's children. Of course, I know that the three men I'm with never actually really were a part of the community, but they feel familiar.

"Our boss, M, just like in James Bond," Quentin explains. "She wants to meet you. We tried to get her to wait, but she's the one who decides what happens next, so it's better if we comply. But don't worry, she's pretty nice."

"And once she eats my biscuits, she'll agree to whatever we want," Leek boasts. To be honest, after eating mine, I tend to agree. These biscuits are sin.

The living room is nothing special. Two sofas, a TV, a low table that's full of empty crisp bags and scattered files. The bookcases on the walls are empty, another sign that this is only a temporary place to stay. There's a few board games on the bottom shelf of one of them, tattered and slightly yellowed from the sunlight streaming in through the large window. Leek has taken his hands off the wheelchair handles, so I use the opportunity to wheel myself to the window and take a look outside. A field, endless and green. This could be anywhere, but at least I now know that we're in a very rural place. There's a few white spots in the distance, sheep maybe.

The men let me be, luckily. As boring as the view is at first sight, it is relaxing at the same time. The sun is shining, surrounded by fluffy white clouds.

"She needs clothes," Leek announces to the other two. "Think Mrs M can bring some? I wouldn't have a clue what to buy."

"Good idea. Laya, anything in particular you want?"

I turn away from the window. What am I supposed to say? I don't want to be relying on them. I don't want to be in their debt, but I do need something to wear.

"Something simple. Modest."

Quentin nods and begins to type a message on his phone. A moment later, it beeps.

"She asks what colours you like?"

In the village, we all wore white clothes, simple, uniform. We didn't want individuality, and we didn't need clothes to express ourselves. Colours would have only distracted from our devotion to the Angel.

"White, please, if that's not too much trouble," I reply quietly. Their smiles slip a little and I know that I've reminded them once again that I'm different. That I don't belong in this world where people care about how they look.

The phone beeps again. "Trousers or skirts?" Quentin asks.

I'm about to say skirts, but then I remember that I'm living with three men. Skirts are feminine, they might give the wrong expression. I'll feel safer in trousers. I trust them, mostly, but I've been taught to be cautious. Andros told us how men outside the community have become more violent towards women and less inhibited. That the laws were changed to make it easier for men to do what they want. Women in this society are suppressed, that's what he's said. That's why living in the village was so much better, where there were clear rules of how men and women had to behave in the rare occasions they interacted.

"Trousers."

Quentin frowns for a moment but then nods and types yet another message. "What's your size?"

"I have no idea. I used to be a size twelve, but I think I've lost weight since then."

"You certainly have," Andrew mutters under his breath, just loud enough for me to hear. Does he think I'm too thin? Well, after looking at myself in the mirror yesterday, he's probably right.

"That's fine, she's got pictures to look at. And Laya doesn't want anything formfitting anyway, right?"

I shake my head.

"Shoe size?"

That Mrs M seems to be asking a lot of questions.

"Six." I don't think that has changed. Not that I'm used to wearing shoes anymore. Right now, I'm wearing socks because someone put them on me, but usually I'm barefoot. When we first started doing that, it was a little painful on the rough ground, but the skin on the soles of my feet hardened quickly until it only hurt when I accidentally stepped on a particularly sharp rock.

"She says she's going shopping now and will be here in two hours."

Leek looks at his watch. "It's 10.42 right now. Bet she's going to be here at 12.42 exactly?"

Andrew laughs. "I'm not going to take that bet. We all know she's going to." He turns to me with a grin. "M is very precise. Unless she wants to surprise people, then she's the opposite."

"What are we going to do for the next two hours?" Leek asks. "I could make lunch, although that will depend on whether I can figure out how the hob works. Laya, anything you want to do?"

"Shower," I say immediately. "I'd like to take a shower. Is that allowed today?"

They all stare at me as if I said something really, really sad.

Twenty-Two

Mrs M looks like a stereotypical grandmother. White hair propped up in a bun, warm eyes surrounded by tiny wrinkles, laughing lines on the corners of her lips. She's not the thinnest, but she's not overweight either. Average, I'd say. And just like the men predicted, she's at our front door at 12.42 exactly. I wonder if she stood there for a few minutes and waited for the precise moment to ring the doorbell.

"Dearie, so good to meet you," she says as soon as Quentin leads her into the kitchen where the rest of us are waiting. "I got you some clothes, want me to help you put some on?"

Without waiting or even greeting Andrew and Leek, she takes the wheelchair handles and pushes me out of the room, towards the bathroom.

"Can't have you sit around in pyjamas all day. I'm going to have a word with the boys, mind you, not thinking of this earlier. They're supposed to be clever."

She huffs and continues chatting away without

expecting me to reply. "They're good at their jobs, but sometimes they lack a bit of common sense. I got you some nice shower gel as well, they probably have one smelling all masculine. You don't need shampoo at the moment, but I'll get you some soon, once your hair has grown back a little."

"I don't want it to grow," I say quietly.

I expect her to protest, like the men probably would, but she continues in the same chatty tone as before. "That's fine, darling, I'll organise a razor for you. And if you want a wig at some point, just let me know. For now, it's important that you stay inside, but once we have things under control, you might want to go outside without standing out."

As much as the sunlight calls to me, the thought of going outside scares me. There will be people everywhere. It was hard enough in hospital with all the doctors, nurses, police officers, but there will be a lot more people now. And Mrs M is right, I will stand out like a sore thumb with my gaunt face and my shorn scalp. Maybe they'll think I'm a cancer patient, but even so, they'll notice me.

"When will you have things under control?" I ask in the hope that she may be more generous with her information than the men.

"It's too soon to say. This has turned out to be much bigger than we expected; much, much bigger. There's a lot of money involved and where there's money, there is trouble."

"That's what my husband used to say," I tell her without thinking. "That's why we didn't use money in the village. There wasn't bartering, either. If someone needed something, it was given to them without wanting something in return."

Mrs M sighs. "Sometimes, I wish society worked that way, but sadly it's more complex than that. I assume you got some things from outside your village though? Clothing? Kitchen supplies?"

"They were donations," I explain, but she tsks.

"Dearie, after looking through the community's accounts, I can assure you that they weren't donations. But let's leave that for another time."

She closes the bathroom door behind us and steps in front of me, holding up two different shirts. "Which one do you prefer?"

When we return to the kitchen, I'm dressed in a white tunic that covers my arms to the wrist, and white linen trousers that are a lot softer against my skin than the fabric I'm used to. She wanted to give me shoes as well, but for now, I'm staying inside the flat, so I told her I didn't need them. So many things are changing around me, and I feel like I'm losing control. Staying barefoot is one tiny thing that I can decide myself.

Leek has made a delicious casserole and while we eat, Mrs M entertains us with stories from her job in a cafe. Apparently, there's a cafe in the centre of Edinburgh that's secretly an outpost of SOCA, where undercover agents can report their findings and get new instructions. One day a week, M works there, even though that's far below her pay grade.

"I make the best hot chocolate in town," she grins when she's emptied her plate. "But I need to be careful, the cafe has now appeared on tourist sites on the internet, and I don't want too many people coming there. But yes, my hot chocolate is legendary. One girl actually moaned when she drank some yesterday."

"You should give me the recipe," Leek suggests cheekily.

"So that you can open your own cafe and take all my guests? I don't think so, young man."

I smile when she calls him a young man. I don't know his age, but I don't think he's anything younger than early thirties, same as the other two. I'd say Quentin is the oldest, but maybe that's just because he acts with the most authority.

"Once you've retired and can't fire me anymore, I'm going to make a joke about your age," Leek grumbles, then winks at me. I love it when he winks.

"You'll have to wait quite a while for that because I have no intentions of retiring. Now, shall we get to work?"

Leek mutters something under his breath while he starts clearing up the plates that we've already stacked in a pile. I feel like I should be helping him, but the wheelchair makes that difficult. Suddenly, I'm noticing how tired I am again. I've been out of bed for several hours now, and I'm feeling the effect. I stifle a yawn, but Andrew notices it.

"How about I bring you back to your room, Laya? I think you could do with a nap."

"No." I shake my head. "I want to stay."

"Darling, you look like you're about to fall out of your chair," Mrs M says cheerily but not without authority. "Go to bed, and if I'm gone by the time you wake up, I give the boys full permission to share anything important with you. Now, off to bed."

I'm too tired to even protest. The energy I had this

morning has disappeared and all that's left is a deep exhaustion. Not just physical, emotional as well. I need a break from all this.

Andrew helps me back into bed and even brings me a glass of water.

"Ring the bell if you need anything, alright? We'll be just next door, and when you wake up, we can tell you if there's something you need to know." He turns around at the door one last time. "Sleep well. You're safe here."

Andros is calling me. He's ordering me to come to him. I walk over broken glass, leaving a trail of blood in my wake. He's somewhere at the other end and I need to get to him.

"Laya!"

He continues to call and I begin to run, flying over the broken dreams I'm walking on.

"Pain is salvation! Come to me, Princess!"

His voice has taken on that special tone that means that I'll be punished if I don't immediately do as he says. I run faster, even though I know that the skin on my feet is cut into pieces.

"Faster! They're catching up with you!"

I look over my shoulder and there are other people running behind me, chasing me. I can't see who they are, but they feel familiar. Maybe I should wait and see if they're a threat.

"They want to turn you. I can see the attraction you feel

for them! Come now before you're torn away from the Angel!"

The Angel. His light is bright on the horizon, beckoning me closer. Andros is standing beneath it, drenched in golden light. He holds his arms out to me.

"Come, my wife. Let us be one in front of the Angel."

I look back one more time, but the three figures aren't coming any closer. I've been too fast for them.

I reach Andros, panting and bloodied, and collapse in front of him. My legs can no longer carry me. He bends down and takes my face in his hands, cupping my cheeks in the way he always used to. Like I'm his, forever his.

"You've come back to me, sweet Laya," he whispers and presses small kisses on my forehead. "Now we're ready to be together, forever. Only one last thing to do and then we can meet the Angel."

Suddenly, he's wielding an iron tong that's holding a flaming golden crown. The gold is quivering in the heat, threatening to melt and drip onto the ground. He lowers it and I realise what he's about to do.

"You can't ascend until you're broken, my little bird. I will have to break your wings before they can regrow in the Angel's light."

I shriek and scramble away from him, but he's too strong. He's got one hand around my neck, ready to snap it if I don't comply. I'm just a lost little bird to him, one he can kill and maim at his heart's content.

The golden crown is getting closer to my head, bubbling and burning. It will sear my flesh and merge with me. I will be Andros's Princess forever, bound to him by a shackle visible to all. There will be no freedom even in Paradise.

A drop of molten gold drips down on my shorn scalp and I scream in agony.

"Scream for me," Andros whispers and lowers the crown until it almost touches my head. The heat is unbearable, singing the tiny hairs that have escaped the last shave. Then, he opens the tongs and lets the crown fall. It swallows me whole in more pain than I've ever experienced.

"Now you're mine, my broken little Princess."

Twenty-Three

I can't stop screaming. Pain is in my skull, in my neck, everywhere. I wrap my hands around my head, shielding me from the pain, but it only makes it worse. There's no escape. Andros won't stop until I'm truly broken, truly his. All he needs to do now is extinguish the last tiny flicker of doubt, and then I'll be his forever.

"It's just a nightmare," someone calls, but I know that isn't true.

It's real, so very real. His grip on me is tight, the bloody crown only the latest sign of his power over me. I'll never be free. He's merged himself with me, fused ourselves together. He's always with me, just like the band around my ankle. I can't remove him without removing too much of myself.

"Come with me," Andros hisses. "You're mine. They can't give you what you need."

I pull away from him, trying to escape his grip. The pain is getting worse, but I know that I can't stay. He's not going to let me go once we've ascended. He's broken my wings and he's not going to let them grow again. He's going to keep me caged, no matter whether we're on Earth or in Paradise.

"Let me go," I whimper, bracing myself against the next wave of pain that he'll throw at me. He's relentless, torturing me just because he can. There's no point to it all. It has nothing to do with ascension, with the Angel. It's all about him, Andros, and his desire to own me.

I push him away with all my might. "No more," I whisper, ripping the crown off my head.

"That's it! Fight him!"

Voices from far away, familiar and kind. I cling to the hope they give me, no matter whether they're real or not. Is Andros real? Or the voices? Or nothing at all? Maybe I'm dead already, stuck in between life and Paradise. Maybe I have to prove myself here before I'm allowed to continue. Or is this hell, where Andros gets to torture me for eternity?

"Don't fight me, sweet little girl. You're mine and you know it. Put on that crown again."

The Prophet's voice is soft and alluring, soothing me into doing what he wants. I look down at the crown. My hands are full of smeared gold and burn marks, but they hold it tight, not letting it fly back onto my head. It's struggling though, wriggling in my grip. I can't stop it much longer.

"You're strong, Laya. Remember how strong you are."

It's one of the three, I know that now. The three shadows who I thought were chasing me, but in fact they were trying to rescue me. Now they're saying that I'm strong. Do I believe them?

"They're wrong," Andros whispers into my ear. "You're weak, you're broken. Nobody can help you, least of all them. They lied to you, they betrayed you. They took you away from me."

That was the wrong thing to say. "Yes, they did." I look him straight in the eyes. "And that's all I've wanted. I no longer want to be with you. You're cruel and I don't think the Angel will ever welcome you into his Paradise. That's why you do it. You're bitter and you want to prevent the rest of us from being happy." He's gasping for words, but before he can reply, I throw the burning crown at him and it lands on his head, crushing his skull as he cries in pain.

"Pain is salvation," I say softly as I'm ripped away from him and into the waiting arms of the people who actually care for me.

I wake lying on the floor, looking up at three very concerned faces. I lift a hand and touch my forehead. No crown. No blood.

"He's gone," I whisper hoarsely. "I made him go away. I saw him for what he was. I looked into his soul and saw only darkness."

I notice only now that I'm cradled in someone's arms. Quentin. His gaze is soft as he looks down at me. All of them are watching me cautiously, as if they're scared that I might do something crazy again.

"I'm okay now," I tell them. "I fought him."

Andrew clears his throat. "Fought who?"

"Andros. He tried to break me, and I fought and won. I got away and left him."

"It was just a dream, right?" Leek says slowly, as if to make sure that I haven't gone completely bananas. "You know that?"

I smile. "Believe me, it was so much more than that. But why am I on the floor?"

Quentin grimaces. "You screamed and I came to see what was wrong. You were flailing in bed and I was worried you might hurt yourself, so I tried to hold you still... Well, you pushed me back, I fell and dragged you with me."

"It looked quite hilarious, now that I know you're safe," Andrew says with a chuckle. "You toppling Quentin. He's usually pretty good in a fight."

I roll to one side and groan as pain tells me that it's not a good idea.

"You may have hurt yourself falling. Where is the pain?" Andrew's expression has changed to that of the doctor, all business, but there's concern in his eyes.

"I'm fine, just some bruises. Nothing I can't handle," I mutter. "Help me up?"

"Sure?" Andrew is locking his eyes with mine, examining me closely.

"Yes, yes, everything's fine."

Quentin gently shifts his position behind me and pushes me up, out of his lap. He steadies me until I can sit by myself, without my head spinning too much.

"Do you want to go back to bed?" he asks but I immediately shake my head. No, I don't think I want to face any more dreams just now. I'm quite happy to be awake and deal with reality.

"No, I need to think. But I also don't want to be alone right now."

"We'll stay," Andrew says immediately. "Unless you only want one of us?"

I smile at him. His warmth is just what I need. It feels greedy and selfish, but I can't help but whisper, "All of you."

"Let's make you more comfortable first," Quentin says from behind me. "Want to go back on the bed? Not to sleep, just so you can sit a little better than on the floor?"

I nod. He wraps his arms around me and picks me up, depositing me on the bed before sitting down beside me. He touched me, he carried me, but for some reason, I don't mind. I actually liked it.

"Could I have some paper and a pen?" I ask, having an idea all of a sudden. Leek disappears from the room and comes back a moment later, carrying a large scrapbook and a handful of pens.

"That was the first I could find," he shrugs as I inspect the assortment of pens. They're all sorts of colours, but not a single black, normal one.

Andrew sits down on my other side, and Leek takes a seat on the other bed. I shouldn't be happy that all three of them are here with me, but they give me strength, make me feel safe. How quickly things have changed.

I open the scrapbook and write my name in the middle of the page and surround it with a circle. Me, the centre of it all. Above me, in a far bigger circle, I place the Angel, and between him and me, I write Andros's name. My hand shakes a little when I do that. No, remember, you're not scared of him anymore. You know him for what he is. A liar. Your enemy.

I notice how quiet the room has become and look up.

They're all watching me. I grimace and wiggle further back until I'm leaning against the wall. Hopefully, they won't be able to see what I'm drawing now. Quentin's eyes are following my every move and there's a twitch to his lips that looks like he wants to say something.

"It's private," I tell them before he gets the chance.

"We're not looking," Andrew promises, "But could I have some paper as well?"

I shrug and rip out a page for him. He turns until he faces me, then begins to draw, using a book he's picked up from under the bed as a table. He purposely turns the paper so I can't see what he's doing, but I guess that's exactly what I'm doing as well.

I continue my work and add the men's names towards the bottom of the sheet, and below them, Mrs M and SOCA. Now I've got all the main players. I'm not even sure why I'm doing this, but it feels important. My head is so full of emotions, images, worries, that I need to let them out somehow.

I take a green pen – green, the colour of hope – and start scribbling random words around the circled names. What I feel about them. What I'm scared of. What might happen if I let them close.

Putting it all on paper gives my mind space to think. I quickly draw some lines connecting some of the words. Yes. It's beginning to make sense. I open a new page and write the Angel's prayer in the centre.

Discipline leads to redemption.
Suffering brings peace.
Obedience inspires happiness.

Pain is salvation.
The Angel is our shield and our refuge.

It's so familiar and yet, it's started to feel strange. Andros has used this prayer to turn us into his slaves. He's taken something beautiful and changed it into something evil.

I take a red pen and scratch out most of the words.

~~Discipline leads to~~ *redemption.*
~~Suffering brings~~ *peace.*
~~Obedience inspires~~ *happiness.*
~~Pain is~~ *salvation.*
The Angel is our shield and our refuge.

Yes, that's better. That's the essence of my belief in the Angel. I don't believe he wants us to suffer. No, I believe that he wants to deliver us from suffering. Not just in Paradise, but here on Earth. Redemption, peace, happiness, salvation.

I smile at the thought of how a few changes have turned it into something positive.

One last thing to do. I scribble down the rules of the community. The ones that I've been following for years. Clothing, demeanour, gender separation, schedules, food. There are so many rules that I only have space to write the most important ones. The more I note down, the tenser I feel. I've been constricted by them for so long that they feel like family. Not the good kind of family though. I want to free myself from them, but it's not easy to leave your family behind. I'll have to do it step by step, and I will need help. I see that now. I can't do it all on my own.

I mark a few of the rules with coloured dashes, then look up. Quentin and Leek are still watching me, but Andrew is busy drawing something. He lifts his gaze from the paper. There's a slight sheen of red spreading across his cheeks. Is he embarrassed?

"Show us," Leek demands and gets up from his bed, as if he's about to take the drawing by force, if necessary.

"It's private," the doctor protests, but Leek snaps the paper out of his hand.

"Laya is allowed privacy. You aren't." He steps back and looks at the drawing, his eyes widening. "Oh."

"Give it back!" Andrew complains, but he's smiling.

"Leek," Quentin commands playfully. "My turn."

With a grin, Leek turns the paper over, and because I'm sitting next to Quentin, I finally get to see it. It's me. Not Laya, the Prophet's Princess, but me, how I'd like to be. Confident and strong and sane. It's only a rough sketch, but the detail is amazing. My eyes are lively and my cheeks are a healthy colour, not as gaunt as they are now. My lips are curved in a gentle smile which almost makes me want to smile back. He's only drawn the face and neck so far, not the hair. Is he going to keep my scalp bald, or is he going to add hair, like there used to be?

"Can I?" Andrew asks sharply and pulls the drawing out of Quentin's hand. "It's not finished."

He takes another pen and continues his work, while I'm left confused. And maybe a little flattered.

"Laya?" Quentin's voice is gentle and so warm that it reaches all the way into my heart.

"Yes?"

"You looked a little spaced out for a moment. Everything alright?"

"Yes." I take a deep breath and look back at all the notes I've made. "I'd like to have a chat with all of you. Not here though."

They look at me curiously, but nobody protests. Andrew puts away his drawing and helps me back into the wheelchair. Together, we head to the living room. I'd intended to stay in the chair, but Leek lifts me up and deposits me on one of the soft sofas. He even puts a blanket around me and sits down on the sofa next to me. I feel teary when I consider how gentle he is with me. This large man who could probably squash my skull with one hand, is covering me with a blanket, as if I'm too frail to do it myself. Well, maybe I am.

They look at me expectantly. I take a deep breath. This isn't going to be easy.

"This might be a little weird," I begin, "but I have a few things I want to say. Can you promise not to interrupt? I don't know if I'll be able to finish otherwise."

"Of course," Quentin says with a reassuring smile. "We're listening."

I nod and gather my thoughts. So much to say, my brain is a little overwhelmed. "First of all, I'd like to testify against Andros. I'm sorry I didn't say so from the beginning, but it's taken me a while to figure things out."

Leek's expression lights up and I suppress a smile.

"Next, I would like your help to... become more normal again. I don't want to let go of my principles or of my beliefs, but I don't want to feel like an alien on a different planet. I need to get used to interacting with normal people. If you touch me, I don't want to feel as if you're about to hurt me. I want to sit next to one of you without feeling horrible about it because you're men and I'm a woman. I want to wear something colourful. I want to shower every day and I want you to stop me if I ask for permission for it. And I want you to try and remove the metal from my ankle, even if that means you'll have to amputate my foot. I want it gone."

I go over my mental list. I'm sure I've forgotten half of what I was aiming to say. "Basically, I want to be like I used to be, except that I'll be different as well. I learned a lot and I found something to believe in, even if some of it was wrong. I don't want to erase all my bad memories, but I want to learn to live with them, and learn from them. Does that make sense at all?"

So far, they've been quiet, listening intently, but now they all start speaking at the same time. All the confidence I felt moments ago drains from me and I pull my legs to my chest, making myself small.

"Do you want a hug?" Leek whispers, his breath touching my cheek. Do I? Everything inside of me is screaming for warmth and comfort, but am I ready for this? Will I be able to stand his touch without wanting to push him way?

"Yes. I would like a hug."

Epilogue

TWO MONTHS LATER.

I lift Leek's arm from my chest and slip out of bed. He's still fast asleep, and I know better than to wake him. He's very grumpy in the mornings, at least until he's either had some tea or something to eat. Preferably both.

I walk to the bathroom and take a long shower. At the beginning, I hurried to wash myself, but now, it's become an indulgence. Part of the healing process, Quentin says. I'm going against some of the old rules, but not in a destructive way. I wash my hair and breathe in the sweet coconut scent of the shampoo. I'm letting my hair grow, although I'm planning to keep it quite short. I don't want to be vain; all I want is to blend in, and I can't do that with a shorn head. Again, another compromise. I'm getting quite good at them. I've progressed to wearing more colourful clothes, although I'm still keeping them modest. I won't be showing my cleavage any time soon. And why should I? It's my body and I get to decide who sees it. For now, that's only me and three other people. In moderation.

Someone knocks at the door. "Do you need much longer?"

"Yes!" I shout back with a grin. There's a second bathroom, so it's not like Quentin is going to have to pee into a bucket. The shower in this one is much better though, so it's everybody's favourite.

We're in a new safe house, a more permanent one this time. Leek was a little sad that the kitchen was smaller, but at least he finds the hob easier to use. He's started taking cookery classes, which has the added side effect of us getting to try out some rather exotic dishes. Nothing compared to the meagre and bland food I got back at the compound. I've gained some weight, although Andrew tells me it's still not enough. I try and eat more, but I've also taken up self-defence classes with Quentin, which burn quite a lot of calories. Leek keeps me supplied with brownies though, and once he's taken me to Mrs M's cafe to try her hot chocolate. She wasn't lying when she said that it was the best in Scotland.

I step out of the shower and wrap my head in a towel. There's a mirror, but I ignore it. That's one thing I still have to learn how to do. Look at my body and recognise myself. At the moment, I see a stranger and that's frightening, more than I want to admit.

I slip into a fluffy bathrobe and matching slippers, and leave the bathroom on the hunt for Andrew. He should be up by now; he's always the first.

I find him in the office, staring at a spreadsheet on the computer. "Are you here to rescue me?"

He sighs and turns around to greet me. He looks tired, but I know he's working on a case that's keeping him up at night. Their main job is still to look after me, but occasionally, Andrew and Quentin get sent case studies to analyse or requests for advice. I've learned not to ask them about details, they're not allowed to tell me anyway.

"Can you do my back?" I ask and hand him a tube of cream. He nods and points to the other office chair in the room. I sit on it the wrong way round so that my chest is against the chair's mesh back. Taking a deep breath, I slide my bathrobe down to give him a full view of my back. I'm always tempted to cover up again and run as soon as I do this, but it's necessary. The scars on my back get itchy if I don't keep them moisturised, and I can't bear to touch them myself. Andrew is the only one allowed to do this, because I can imagine him doing this in his doctor role rather than his friend persona.

"Ready?" he asks calmly and I nod, pressing my teeth together in anticipation of the memories that instantly flood my mind as soon as his fingers touch my back. They're not too bad today, mainly the sensation of Andros's whip, but nothing else. Not his voice, which is a relief. A week ago, I started crying when I heard the Prophet speak and it took Andrew half an hour to calm me down. I don't want to be weak, but I know that I'm allowed to be. The three men keep me safe and give me the space I need to recover. I can't believe how lucky I am to have them.

"My husband once told me how humans can only be lucky when they're in Paradise," I tell Andrew randomly, but immediately correct myself. "Sorry, I mean Andros."

It was a shock to find out that the marriage wasn't

actually official. I'd signed something on our wedding day, but nobody at the council was ever notified, so the marriage is null and void. It saves me from having to file for a divorce.

Andros's trial won't be for months, but I've started to give official statements, mostly to my men, sometimes to other police officers. Did I just call them my men? Well, I guess they are. My three protectors, friends, confidants. Partners. Maybe more. They've not only saved me from hell, but also from myself.

"Why do you say that?" Andrew asks with a chuckle. He's used to me saying random things, especially when he does my back. Sometimes, the words burst out of me and I need to say them before they start to hurt. Luckily, he and the others are always willing to listen, even if it's with bemusement at the randomness.

"I just thought how lucky I am to have you," I mutter, a little embarrassed.

He lifts the bathrobe and wraps it around my shoulders again. "And we're lucky to have you. Now, are you brave enough to wake Leek? I'm getting hungry."

I laugh and get off the chair, turning around to look at him. "Thank you."

I leave before he can say anything else. They keep telling me how they want me here, how I'm not a burden in the slightest, and how I'm definitely not just a job. I wish I could show them that I want to be more. They know, but I feel like it needs proof. Hugs are as far as I can go though, and even those not every day. To be honest, I don't know if I'll ever be able to be with them physically. I tried kissing Leek one day, but had to stop. The images and feelings assaulting me were too much. They understand though.

We're a family. Our bond is strong, we don't need the physical bit. I mean, who cares about sex when you can have love?

Not sure that's the right word. We're still fumbling in the dark, trying to define a relationship that's stranger than anything I've ever done before. Three men and me. Brought together by tragedy, but bound by the will to survive.

I head back to the bedroom, where Leek is still snoring softly. I smile to myself and quickly get dressed, taking some random clothes from the wardrobe. I don't really care about what I look like. It needs to be warm and comfortable, that's all that matters to me. Autumn has arrived and the air has turned cooler.

Before I wake Leek, I kneel in front of the small Angel statue in the corner. I no longer say the mantras we were taught. I no longer believe that suffering brings peace. Strangely enough, the absence of suffering right now is bringing me a lot more peace than I ever got while living in the village. The cult. That word is still strange on my tongue. I try and use it, because everyone else does, but it feels wrong. I don't want to say that I was in a cult. Only pliable, weak people join cults, not an educated woman like me. It's humiliating to think of how I was manipulated into being someone so different from who I really am. In retrospective, it's easy to point fingers and see exactly where things went wrong, but life doesn't work that way. Some days, I see things clearly, other days, I need a bit of help with that.

May this be a good day, I ask the Angel. May I be a good person. May the sun shine upon this world. May my men stay safe. May the whole world be at peace.

My prayer has changed a lot. I don't confess sins, I don't ask for punishment. I focus on the positive things in life and hope that the Angel's light will guide me to be a better person. That's what it's all about.

"Good morning," Leek yawns.

"I was supposed to wake you," I complain, bowing in front of the statue one last time. "Couldn't you have waited two minutes?"

"I can go back to sleep if you want. And you could come back to bed, too."

I've developed a strange kind of habit to crawl into one of the guys' beds when it's time to sleep. I get nightmares otherwise. While I'm not good with touch during the day, I need it at night. Leek snores, but he's like a big soft pillow to snuggle against. Andrew likes to hold me close, as if he needs to make sure that I'm still there. He snores sometimes, too. Quentin tosses around a lot, and sometimes wakes up in the middle of the night, but he says it's just the stress of his work that makes it hard for him to sleep well.

"Come on, why are you up yet? It's too early." Leek yawns again, showing me his blinding white teeth. He's dyed his hair bright red and is trying to convince me to do the same. No chance.

"I'm going to get my new identity today," I tell him excitedly. I'd almost forgotten. My new name. It's taken longer than expected, but now I'm ready to officially start this new life. New home, new name, new beginning.

"Ah yes. I hope you'll like it."

I look at the clock on the wall. "You've got six minutes

until M arrives. Better hurry up, I don't think she'll appreciate seeing you half naked."

"You never know," he mutters, but finally gets out of bed.

"I'll be in the kitchen," I tell him and leave before he starts getting changed. Seeing naked men? Still not a good idea.

I make tea for the five of us and wait. A new name. The men made some suggestions to M, but in the end, someone else decides. I have no idea what it'll be. It could be something dreadful like Harriet. There will be two first names and a surname, a fake date of birth and all the documents I need to register a bank account, pay taxes and all that sort of stuff. For now, I'm stuck at home, not allowed to go outside on my own, but I'm planning to get a job as soon as I can.

Last week, they caught two men who they think were being paid to assassinate members of the Angel's community. After Eamon and his wife, three more were found dead, but so far, nobody knows if they took their own lives to reach ascension or if someone killed them. Andros hasn't said a word since being taken to prison, and I know him well enough to suspect that he won't be pleading guilty either. He doesn't see anything wrong in what he did. What I really want to know is if he's really responsible for the killings.

The doorbell rings - four short times, two long - but before I can get there, Quentin lets in Mrs M. The old lady is carrying a leather briefcase, making it very clear that this is an official visit. As much as she likes to joke with the men, she's still their boss.

The other two join us around the kitchen table, but before I can ask about my new identity, M pulls out two photos from her bag.

"Ever seen these two men, Laya?"

I take a good look at them, but they don't seem familiar. Neither of them looks very friendly.

"No, why?"

"One of them was a porter at the hospital you stayed at. Well, he pretended to be a porter, but in reality, he's a wanted criminal. We finally got him. And, you'll like this bit, he's given us a lot of information. Most of our theories were correct. There's a kill list making the rounds with the names of most of the former Angel cult members. Andros invested some of their money while you were living in the village, and it seems he's more than doubled the collective money pot. Of course, that means more people are interested in getting their hands on it."

"Does that mean Laya is still in danger?" Quentin asks sharply, earning himself a frown from M.

"I was getting to that. As a result of the confession we got from the fake porter, a court order is currently being processed to dissolve the company Andros created. That means all the money people gave to him will be paid back, despite the contracts that you all signed. I've arranged for your portion to be transferred onto the bank account set up under your new name, Laya."

"So, I've got money now?" I'm a bit confused by all this news. I was expecting to get my new identity, nothing more.

M chuckles. "Yes, and quite a bit. It'll help start your new life, once all this is over. There's no date set for the trial yet, but I guess it's going to be a few more months, so you've got time to make plans. But for now, I think you're safer than you have been in quite a while."

"We're not leaving her," Andrew says almost angrily. "She stays with us."

M holds up her hands. "I never said you have to. You'll be assigned to her until the trial is over, at the very least." She winks at me. "Don't worry, you won't lose your knights in shining armour any time soon."

"And you won't lose us after the trial either," Leek whispers. My belly fills with warmth at their words. It's good to have a home, a family. People who want me.

At first, Mrs M had been against the burgeoning relationship between me and the men, but she's finally changed her mind. I know it's not supposed to be this way, it should be just a job for them, but if she was to split us up, she probably knows that we'd just find a way to get together again. We're a team, a family.

M takes out a large envelope from her briefcase and slides it over the table until it's right in front of me. "Here's your new life."

I breathe in deep, trying to get the shaking under control that has started to creep up on me. My fingers are trembling as I open the envelope and pull out several documents and a passport.

"If you don't like it, we can continue calling you Laya," Quentin promises, knowing exactly what's running through my head. "Or you choose a different name. Who cares what it says on paper."

M clears her throat but doesn't say anything.

With shaking hands, I open the passport.

Valerie Eleanor Dawn.

Leek peeks over my shoulder. "Ellie!"

"Valerie means strength and Eleanor means light," M explains over Leek's shout. "I think dawn is self-explanatory."

Valerie. Eleanor. Dawn.

Ellie.

I turn to my men and smile.

"Hi, my name is Ellie. Want to have an amazing new life with me?"

This book is part of the Defiance series, a set of standalone novels combining reverse harem romance with real life issues, all featuring SOCA and Mrs M.

Stay in this world by reading Frozen Heart, a contemporary romance set on the streets of Edinburgh, Scotland.

skyemackinnon.com/defiance

Newsletter
skyemackinnon.com/newsletter

Frozen Heart Sample

Read on for a sample of Frozen Heart, part of the Defiance Series, a trilogy of standalone novels all dealing with social issues.

CAN SHE TRUST THE MEN PROMISING TO SAVE HER?

Emily never expected to find herself on the street and looking for a place to stay. A park bench doesn't seem very inviting in the depths of winter.

Her luck changes when a mysterious stranger offers her shelter. It seems too good to be true, and when she meets his other two house mates, she starts to question if he's the good Samaritan he seems to be.

Staying means things she couldn't even dream of, but could mean a broken heart if the dream shatters. Going means facing the dangers of the winter streets. Can she make the impossible choice? And will she make the right one?

One

I was riding my girlfriend's strap-on when she told me to move out.

Six weeks later, I'm living on the streets. I wish we'd split up in the summer. Edinburgh in winter is fucking cold. There's no snow, but the icy wind is blowing straight through my thin trench coat. Oh yes, did I mention my ex also threw away all my stuff when I didn't collect it immediately? Hell, I didn't have anywhere to live yet, I was staying at friends' houses mostly. There was no space to put a dozen cardboard boxes. So, she threw it out without telling me. Bitch.

I don't even know why we were still together. I should have moved out ages ago. I guess it became a habit, living together, her paying the rent, me paying for everything else. Sleeping together. Fighting. Hurting. Bruising, occasionally.

Now I'm without a girlfriend, without a flat, without a job. At the beginning, I took my laptop to cafes and pubs to use their free Wi-Fi but, after a while, the money I spent on drinks was more than the money I earned with my freelance translating. It's a dead job. Nowadays, people use the internet to translate their stuff. And the quick birth certificate translations I get through the agency don't pay enough to survive on. Now my laptop is at my friend Ali's house, where I stayed for a week until her parents came for a visit. For a whole fucking month. I should be grateful that I could sleep on her sofa for as long as I did, but it hurts that I'm now sitting on a cold park bench while my friends are in their flats and houses, warm, cosy, happy.

My two other friends here in Edinburgh are saying that I could stay with them again, but one of them's got a baby and no space, and the other has OCD. I stayed at her place for a night, but I saw how stressful it was for her to have someone else in her sanctuary, so I wouldn't want to do that to her again.

I should have made more friends. Three friends, that's all I've got. My girlfriend didn't like me spending time with other people, especially women. She was always the jealous type but, at the beginning, I found it endearing. It made me feel special. Now, I wish I'd seen those signs for what they were. I should have left her long ago, on my terms, with a new place to live sorted out and a moving van to take my stuff there. Instead, the opposite happened. She threw me out and now I'm lost, drifting while trying to find my feet.

Maybe I'll get a place in the hostel tonight. I sigh and watch my breath slowly disappear into the morning air. The sun is trying to break through the hanging clouds and its meek light is touching the frosty grass around me. I'm in the centre of town, on a strip of park running right along busy Princes Street. From here, I can see the old town, its tall stone houses that huddle together on the volcanic rock, leading up to the imposing castle at one end and down to the parliament on the other. It's a beautiful view, one that every tourist captures when they come here. Even now, early in the morning, they are everywhere, conquering the city for themselves, outnumbering the locals on their way to work.

A fine mist covers the city, but it's not raining. Yet. It's true what they say about Scottish weather. It's terrible. It makes you really appreciate the sun when it can be bothered to shine a little. At the moment, it's still fighting for dominance with the clouds. Maybe later.

I watch people hurry by me, not sparing me a second glance. Dark coats, gloves, and in the case of the less fashion-conscious, woollen hats. They're all dressed for winter, even though they'll soon be in their warm offices, working away like the busy bees they are. I've never been one to work nine to five, but right now, I crave it. Better than sitting here, not doing anything.

I sigh and get up, shaking my frozen legs. Maybe sitting on a cold bench wasn't the best idea. But there are not enough tourists here yet to make begging worth it.

I hate it. I fucking hate it. Never thought I'd be begging for money. I've got a university degree – which also got me into debt, so there are no savings that could carry me over.

I have an overdraft, debts and no cash whatsoever. I thought about selling my laptop, but it's the only way I might still be able to find work again. For now, begging is the only way to survive. Two quid is enough to get me a few hours' warmth in a café with a hot drink. Luckily, they let me in, unlike some of the other rough sleepers. I don't look homeless yet, and hopefully I don't smell it either. I give my armpits a doubtful sniff. Could be worse. The church I stayed at last night didn't have a shower, but if I get a space in the hostel, I'll be able to have a quick one tonight. Using their totally masculine smelling menthol shampoo. But I'm not one to be choosy right now. Even if I smell like a fifty-year-old guy with dandruff.

At the hostel, I'll also get to give my clothes a quick wash. I've got a few more tops and one pair of jeans stored with Ali, but I'm trying to keep them for when my current ones start falling apart. I'm planning long term now. At the beginning, I thought it would only be a night or two until I'd find somewhere to stay. But then I missed an appointment with the council because the bus broke down, and now they're not seeing me as a priority. They told me I could move in with my parents again. Yeah, as if that's going to happen. They threw me out when I was sixteen, so I don't think they'd be pleased to take me in now. Maybe they won't even notice if I don't call them for Christmas this year. I'm certainly not going to spend any money on phoning them if I could spend it on a hot chocolate.

A drop of rain lands on my cheek. The sun has lost its battle. I better move, otherwise all the sheltered spots will be gone. Beggars *can* be choosy.

I grab my backpack, grimace at the dirt it's covered in, and head towards the Royal Mile, where it's easiest to get noticed by tourists.

I keep my head down. I pretend I'm not, but I'm ashamed.

I find a spot in a covered archway close to the parliament. There are not many tourists here yet – most go to the Castle first before they head down to Holyrood Palace and the parliament – but sometimes the politicians and civil servants like to do a good deed on their way to work and give me a few pennies. That's what I learned straight away: the richer the person in front of me, the less they will put into my bowl. They only do it to feel virtuous, like the good samaritans they certainly are not.

The rain is getting heavier and a few drops find their way onto my clothes, but it's not bad enough yet to venture away from the Royal Mile. This is the most lucrative spot in the entire city. I grimace. Lucrative, what a strange word to use. It's almost like I'm looking at the begging like a business, but that's just wrong. This is only to carry me over until I get my next council appointment and hopefully end up on their list of emergency accommodation. I still can't believe they're not giving me any support. I always thought that people living on the streets only had themselves to blame. That they didn't want help or couldn't be bothered to ask for assistance. Now, my opinion on that has changed. I want help, but nobody is giving it to me, no matter how much I ask for it. I shudder when I remember the cold, uncaring eyes of the woman at the council. She didn't care that my bus had broken down. She didn't care that I had nowhere to go. She just gave me an appointment and made me feel like I should be grateful to only have to wait for six weeks. She's probably sitting in her cosy office just now, looking forward to going home tonight and relaxing in her warm living room. Meanwhile, I'll be freezing my arse off, unless I get a spot in the hostel. In the discarded newspaper I found yesterday, it mentioned snow being expected for the coming days.

More hostels and churches offer beds for the homeless during the winter, but there's still not enough spaces. Someone always has to stay outside, and it's been me several times already. At the beginning, I tried to be nice and let older people move in front of me in the queue, but that altruism is waning quickly. After a sleepless night on a park bench, a grateful smile from a little old lady does nothing to make me warm again. Or dry.

I wrap my arms around my chest, making myself a smaller target for the cold wind that's started to push through the archway. It's a wind channel. Great. No wonder there was nobody else sitting here already.

I peek up at the sky. Dark clouds are gathering above me. I'm not sure if I should be hoping for rain or for snow. Both make the ground wet. Both bring cold that will seep into my bones. I'd love me some sun, but right now, all I can hope for is that these clouds will pass, driven away by Edinburgh's strong sea winds.

Someone drops coins into my bowl and I hurry to look up and smile, but they've already disappeared into the crowd. Good. I hate looking at the people who give me money. They make me feel naked, exposed, dirty. I much prefer for them to stay anonymous.

I lean forward and check the bowl. Not coins. Stones. They actually threw tiny pebbles in there!

My cheeks heat in indignation. As if it wasn't

humiliating enough to sit out here in the cold, no, someone thinks it's funny to put rocks in my bowl. I take them out, revealing the three one pound coins already in there. Two of them are from yesterday. I always try and keep some money behind so it looks as if people have thrown money in my bowl. Somehow, that makes other people add to it. Some kind of weird psychology, I guess, but it also makes me feel better, even though I know that it's not new money.

Three pounds. That's going to buy me a sandwich and a hot tea later on, unless I'm responsible and keep two coins for tomorrow. Then, I'll not even have enough for a coffee.

I grimace and continue to look at the sea of legs rushing past me. They're all full of purpose, rushing towards work or to go sightseeing, who knows? But they all have a destination. I don't. All I can do is sit here and hope that someone will be kind enough to give me a few pennies.

My stomach growls. Fuck. It's going to be a long day.

Two

Two polished leather shoes stop in front of me. I look up – and straight at the crotch of the guy bending down to me. I look away, trying to hide an embarrassed smile. This is as close to a guy as I've come in years. My ex was the jealous type. Which is why I only have three good friends left, all the others let themselves be bullied away. Good riddance. And male friends were taboo – she knew I was bisexual, not just into women like herself, so she saw them as a threat. When I spoke with a guy at a party... not pretty.

"Why are you here?" he asks, and I stare at him.

"What do you think? This piece of pavement feels particularly nice, so I decided to sit here for a few hours."

He sits down next to me, hugging his long legs.

"You're right, this is quite comfortable."

I snort. This guy is crazy. If I could, I'd get up and walk away, but this spot has a roof and a steady stream of people. It's too good to abandon because of a random weirdo.

"What do you want?" I snarl at him, trying to look as

unfriendly as possible. Please leave, I've got enough craziness of my own to deal with.

"Nothing, just taking a break. Walking up the hill is exhausting."

I give him a doubtful look. He's fit, I can tell even though he's wearing a thick leather jacket. There's no way this is guy out of breath from a little stroll up the hill. Edinburgh is full of hills, so if you live here, you get used to it.

"Please, go away," I try more politely this time.

"Why? You haven't answered my question yet."

"Ehm, what?"

"I asked why you're here, and sorry, but this really isn't comfortable." He shifts and his shoulder touches mine in the process. I shiver. Human touch has become a rarity in my life.

"Are you like a street pastor?"

He laughs. "Nah, I don't do God."

I breathe a sigh of relief. I wasn't in the mood for a sermon about what a sinful woman I am, thank you very much. I've had a few of that kind of people try and talk to me over the past weeks. When they offer that I can sleep in their churches for a night, I go with them, endure their speeches, trying to get done with it as soon as possible. If they only want to talk about God without offering me a place to sleep, I tell them to fuck off. Works most of the time.

"If you haven't noticed, I'm homeless. So if you don't want to throw something in my bowl, please move on. You're distracting."

He chuckles. "I know, I can be very distracting." His smile could make any lesser girl faint.

I snort. "Sorry, wrong word. I meant annoying. Now piss off."

"You know you're not very polite?"

"Why should I be? You're invading my privacy."

"If I throw something in your bowl, will you come and get a coffee with me?"

Tempting, but that's creepy. This guy is too friendly. And that usually means trouble. My trust in humanity has suffered a lot since my first night on the streets. Some people think that just because you've got breasts, you're for sale. Or happy to be touched.

"I told you to piss off."

"Come on, it's freezing out here and I really don't want to sit on the cold pavement anymore. I'm in the mood for an americano and a piece of cake. Doesn't that tempt you?"

"I don't go with random men who I don't know," I reply, giving him an evil stare, which he apparently finds amusing.

"Then we better get to know each other." He holds out a gloved hand. "My name is Ben, pleased to meet you."

I don't make any move to take his hand, but he keeps it there, outstretched.

"Go away, Ben," I sigh, but he stays in the same position, grinning like he's the funniest person in the world. The most desperate, maybe. He twitches his fingers, wiggling them one by one.

"Is it the glove that's bothering you? I can take it off."

I sigh again. Why doesn't he get the message?

He takes off his glove and I cringe. His hand is covered in scars, big, fleshy ones. One disappears under the sleeve of his jumper, tempting me to follow it. A silent vulnerability has crept into his eyes, making me think twice about refusing again.

I shake his hand. "I'm Em."

"M, like the letter?"

"Em, like Emily."

"Nice to meet you, Em. Now, how about that coffee?"

"I don't drink coffee. I'm a tea person."

"Tea it is." He gets up and offers me his now gloved hand. I'm about to refuse when I realise I need the loo. Using the toilet in a café beats the public ones by miles. I take his hand and he pulls me up. I sway a little; after sitting in the cold for so long, my feet are frozen. He reaches out to steady me, but I evade him and jump up and down a little, causing him to smile. I stop and glare at him, until he tries to hide his grin.

"There's this cute little coffee shop just around the corner, I go there a lot to work." He points at his messenger bag, bulging with papers and a large laptop.

"What do you do?" I ask, unable to stifle my curiosity.

"This and that," he replies mysteriously. "I can tell you about it in the café."

"You're very persistent, you know that, right?"

"Oh, my flatmates tell me every day."

Flatmates? He looks like he's in his mid-thirties and like he could afford his own place. Who still has flatmates at this age?

We start walking down the Royal Mile, trying to avoid

the groups of tourists huddled together at street corners, listening to their shouting guides.

After a moment of silence, I ask the question that's been hovering on my tongue.

"You have flatmates?"

"Yes, two. Alistair inherited a house and invited us to stay for a summer. It's been four years now, and still working well."

"Don't you want to live on your own?" I loved having my own little flat before I moved in with Jess. Right now, I wish I had somewhere to stay. Even just a room, as long as it was my own, and not shared with crowds of other homeless folks.

"It's a large house, so we can stay out of each other's way if we want, but at the same time, if I want company, I don't need to go far to find it. And this way I don't have to spend a lot of money on rent that I could spend on other things."

"Like what?"

He grins. "Right now, coffee."

He holds open the door of a small café that I almost didn't notice. It's in one of the narrow closes leading off the Royal Mile, one of the darker ones that I wouldn't usually walk through at night. The café looks very inviting though. Candles flicker on the small iron wrought tables, comfy cushions cover the sofas and chairs dotted around the room. And the best thing: it's warm. Roasting, actually.

"May I take your coat?" Ben asks, and I indulge him and let him take it off my shoulders. Apparently, he's got some kind of good Samaritan complex.

He even pulls back my chair when I sit down. A real gentleman. And I still don't know what he wants from me. That worries me more than I want to admit. I hate not knowing.

He orders our drinks from an old lady standing behind a row of cakes and scones, and then sits down opposite me, staring straight into my eyes. I can't help but stare back.

"Have you ever stolen something?" he asks suddenly.

"No," I say automatically before even wondering why he's asking me that question.

"Truth. Interesting."

"Why is that interesting? Not everyone living on the streets is a criminal."

"Obviously." He leans forwards, his elbows pressed on the white table cloth, his index fingers touching his chin. I feel like an animal in the zoo, being stared at curiously. Or, maybe more accurately, a gazelle being ogled by a lion.

"What do you want, Ben?" I sigh, evading his intense brown eyes.

"To get to know you."

"You know, this is really creepy. I think I should go." I move to get up, but the old woman bringing our drinks is in the way.

"Leaving already, dearie?" I look at her tray and see hot chocolate. And sit back down. If it had been tea, I might have been able to leave, but now there's no chance in hell. Hot chocolate is heaven in a mug. With whipped cream on top.

"No, just looking for the toilets."

"Just around the corner, love." I nod my thanks and

follow her directions to a sliding door hiding a single same-sex toilet. I breathe out deeply when I'm finally on my own again, away from Ben. He's strange. Good-looking, almost hot, but very, very strange. I don't get a read on him, and I'm usually good at reading people. He's too friendly. Normally, when people are this friendly, they want something in return. He doesn't look like the type who has to pay for sex. I mean, look at him. He'd just have to chat up a random girl at a party to get a quick fuck, or two. So why is he talking to me? A dirty, unnoticeable street rat?

I take my sweet time, washing my face in the small sink and rubbing some soap on my armpits. Deodorant, Em style. My brown hair is sticky and filthy. I run my hands through it a few times, trying to get the knots out of it. I should probably cut it short, that's more practical for the life I'm currently living. Conditioning my hair is not very high on my list of priorities. My bra is itchy and I'd love to wash it, but I don't want to go back not wearing it. It feels safer with it on, somehow, especially with my shirt being such a thin one.

After another splash of water on my face to wash away the last of the grime, I return to Ben and my hot chocolate. The cream on top of it has started to melt a little, so it's the first thing on my plan of attack. I scoop it up and devour it, savouring the taste of cocoa-covered cream.

Ben watches me with an amused twinkle in his eyes as I delight in slurping the chocolaty foam hiding beneath the cream. I have to come here again, this is the best hot chocolate I've had in years. Then I look at the price written on the large board above the counter and decide not to. At least, not while I still live on the streets. Once I'm back on my own two feet and have a regular income again, I'll come here every day.

I try and pace myself, but suddenly, my mug is empty and Ben is trying to hide a laugh.

"Mary, could we have another hot chocolate, please? Add some marshmallows this time."

Maybe he isn't as bad as I thought at first. I stare at my empty mug, watching tiny brown air bubbles pop their final goodbye on the white porcelain.

"Do you lie?" Ben suddenly asks and I lift my head to stare at him incredulously.

"Seriously? Why are you asking me stuff like that when you could be asking me for my sob story?"

"You didn't answer me when I asked you about that earlier," he says softly.

"Yes, I lie. Not more than everyone else, though. I think."

"Are you a good liar?"

"I guess? It's not something to be proud of, so I've not given it much thought."

He nods. "Let's play a game. Give me three statements about yourself, two truths and one lie, and I'll try and tell them apart."

"No, you start." I don't want to be branded a liar by him.

"Feisty, I like it." He takes a sip from his Americano, which must now surely be cold. "I had a poodle called Mr Fluffy. My favourite colour is black. I have a license to carry a gun."

"The third one."

"Wrong. My favourite colour is pink."

I snort-gasp. "Seriously? That was a second lie."

"Is it?" He smiles mysteriously. "Your turn."

"Okay, let me think. I've never taken drugs. I used to do ballet." I flash my teeth. "I had a Labrador called Mrs Wiggle."

He laughs at the last one. Good. If they laugh, they are more likely to think it's a lie. His smile disappears and he begins to study me, his face suddenly serious.

"Interesting..." he mutters under his breath, but we get interrupted by the woman he called Mary, who's bringing me my second hot chocolate. This time, she's put a heap of tiny marshmallows on the saucer. Perfect. I don't like it when they get soggy.

"The last one," he says confidently.

"Wrong, she really was called that."

"Then the first."

I huff. "Just because I live on the streets doesn't mean that I take drugs, or steal, or lie. This is becoming quite insulting. I never did ballet, I'm not a girly girl, nor have I ever been. I did kickboxing instead."

"Wow, that's unexpected. And useful."

"Useful for what?"

"Mary, could we have some cake?" he calls out instead of answering.

She shuffles over to our little table. "Which one would you like, dearie?" He raises an eyebrow at being called that, but gives her an indulgent smile.

"The raspberry gateau you had last week was delicious. I don't suppose..."

She chuckles. "I've got some in the fridge. I save it for my special customers. And what would you like, darling?"

I look over at the display case filled with the most delicious cakes. "Something with chocolate?"

Ben laughs. "Do you eat anything besides chocolate?"

"Not if I don't have to," I shoot back, my eyes drawn to the large piece of chocolate cake Mary is now placing on a plate.

"Cream?" she asks and I don't find words to reply to this amazing woman.

"Yes, she wants cream," Ben answers her with a chuckle.

Mary takes a glass bowl covered with cling film out of the fridge and reveals a massive portion of whipped cream. Not the cheap bottle stuff, no, the good, fatty, calorific goodness. She puts a generous scoop on my giant piece of cake. I think I'm in heaven.

When Mary puts the plate in front of me, I'm experiencing a food orgasm. Ben looks like he's having fun watching me, but I don't let that deter me from my feast. While he is taking his sweet time with his gateau, my chocolate cake is disappearing at an alarming speed. I will have to brush my teeth extra carefully tonight. The thought of using the public toilets near the station almost drives away my appetite. At night, they are not a place you'd want to be. Smelly, creepy, dark.

"What else do you like besides chocolate?" Ben asks me when I'm finally slowing down a bit.

"Carrots. Spinach. Walnuts." I reply in between chewing on a piece of dark chocolate that found its way into the sponge.

"I didn't mean food, but that's good to know."

"You didn't specify. What food do you like?"

"Sushi," he grins, knowing that I won't be able to resist questioning that.

"But sushi doesn't have chocolate in it. Or is there chocolate sushi?"

"I think you're going to get hyper from all that sugar. Has nobody told you it's not healthy to eat so much sweet stuff?"

"I told you, I also like carrots."

"Which are sweet," he retorts.

"Spinach isn't."

"Okay, spinach is healthy. But you shouldn't eat too much of it, it's got a lot of iron in it."

He looks at me so seriously that I break out in laughter.

"You're not my dietician, so you can piss off."

"Language," he chides and I gape at him.

"Seriously?"

"Seriously," he confirms. "Alistair won't tolerate swearing in his house."

"Well, guess it's good then that I'm not living in his house."

"I was going to-" He breaks off as his phone vibrates in his breast pocket. He checks the caller info and sighs. "I need to take this, wait here."

He goes outside, leaving his jacket behind. It's cold, he'll be freezing. Hopefully it's not a long call. He's walking back and forth, talking agitatedly. I wait a few minutes, sipping the last of my hot chocolate. Then I remember that I still don't know what he wants from me and that it's not safe, so I take my stuff, slip into my coat and sprint out of the cafe while he has his back turned. I hope Mary didn't think I'd stolen anything. Running away probably made me suspicious.

Ben turns when he hears the little bells hanging behind the door, but it's too late, I'm already halfway up the close. I didn't tell him, but I used to be in the running team at school. I'm fast and, right now, I'm running as fast as I can.

Continue reading <u>Frozen Heart</u>, *available in the author's shop, at retailers and in libraries.*

About the Author

Skye MacKinnon is a Scottish romance author who was raised by elves in the mystical Highlands and calls the Loch Ness monster her friend. Her bestselling books weave together romance with action, suspense and whimsical humour, creating page-turners filled with strong heroines, alpha heroes and loveable monsters.

Whether she's writing about aliens in kilts, hunky Vikings or cat shifter assassins, Skye likes to put a new spin on familiar tropes. Some of her heroines don't have to choose, some fall in love with other women, and others get abducted by clueless aliens.

Skye lives with her bossy cat on the west coast of Scotland and uses the dramatic views from her office as an inspiration, no matter whether she writes fantasy, paranormal or science fiction romance. Until she gets abducted by aliens, that is.

Subscribe to her newsletter:
skyemackinnon.com/newsletter

Find all of Skye's books on her website, **skyemackinnon.com**, where you can also order signed paperbacks and swag. Many of her books are available as audiobooks.

PARANORMAL & FANTASY ROMANCE

- **Claiming Her Bears** (post-apocalyptic shifter reverse harem)
- **Daughter of Winter** (fantasy reverse harem)
- **Catnip Assassins** (urban fantasy reverse harem)
- **Infernal Descent** (paranormal reverse harem based on Dante's Inferno, co-written with Bea Paige)
- **Seven Wardens** (fantasy reverse harem co-written with Laura Greenwood)
- **The Lost Siren** (post-apocalyptic, paranormal reverse harem co-written with Liza Street)

SCIENCE FICTION ROMANCE

- **Starlight Highlanders Mail Order Brides** (sci-fi m/f romance, part of the Intergalactic Dating Agency)
- **Starlight Vikings** (sci-fi m/f romance, part of the Intergalactic Dating Agency)
- **Starlight Mermen** (sci-fi m/f romance, part of the Intergalactic Dating Agency)
- **Starlight Monsters** (m/f romance)
- **The Intergalactic Guide to Humans** (sci-fi romance with various pairings)
- **Between Rebels** (sci-fi reverse harem set in the Planet Athion shared world)
- **The Mars Diaries** (sci-fi reverse harem)
- **Through the Gates** (dystopian reverse harem co-written with Rebecca Royce)
- **Aliens and Animals** (f/f sci-fi romance co-written with Arizona Tape)

OTHER SERIES

- **Academy of Time** (time travel academy standalones, reverse harem and m/f)
- **Defiance** (contemporary reverse harem with a hint of thriller/suspense)

STANDALONES

- Song of Souls – m/f fantasy romance, fairy tale retelling
- Wings of Time and Fate - YA fantasy
- Highland Butterflies – lesbian romance

BOX SETS

- Daggers & Destiny – a Skye MacKinnon starter library
- Stars & Seduction - a Sci-Fi Romance starter library